ANTIQUES FLEE MARKET

A TRASH 'N' TREASURES MYSTERY

Antiques Flee Market

Barbara Allan

THORNDIKE
CHIVERS

This Large Print edition is published by Thorndike Press, Waterville, Maine, USA and by BBC Audiobooks Ltd, Bath, England.
Thorndike Press, a part of Gale, Cengage Learning.
Copyright © 2008 by Max Allan Collins and Barbara Collins.
The moral right of the author has been asserted.

LIBRARY OF CONGRESS CATALOGING-IN-PUBLICATION DATA

Allan, Barbara.
   Antiques flee market : a trash 'n' treasures mystery / by
Barbara Allan.
      p. cm. — (Thorndike Press large print mystery)
      ISBN-13: 978-1-4104-1198-3 (hardcover : alk. paper)
      ISBN-10: 1-4104-1198-2 (hardcover : alk. paper)
      1. Large type books. 2. Borne, Brandy (Fictitious
character)—Fiction. 3. Borne, Vivian (Fictitious
character)—Fiction. 4. Mothers and daughters—Fiction. 5.
Antique dealers—Fiction. 6. Antique dealers—Crimes
against—Fiction. 7. Mississippi—Fiction. I. Title.
PS3601.L4A56 2009
813'.6—dc22   2008038942

BRITISH LIBRARY CATALOGUING-IN-PUBLICATION DATA AVAILABLE

Published in 2009 in the U.S. by arrangement with Kensington Books, an imprint of Kensington Publishing Corp.
Published in 2009 in the U.K. by arrangement with The Kensington Publishing Corp.

U.K. Hardcover: 978 1 408 43208 2 (Chivers Large Print)
U.K. Softcover: 978 1 408 43209 9 (Camden Large Print)

Printed in the United States of America
1 2 3 4 5 6 7 12 11 10 09 08

*In memory of Beth Povlsen,
beloved aunt
and bestower of Indian guides*

Brandy's epigraph:
"Three may keep a secret,
if two of them are dead."
Benjamin Franklin

Mother's epigraph:
"There are no secrets better kept
than the secrets that everybody
guesses."
George Bernard Shaw
Mrs. Warren's Profession, Act III

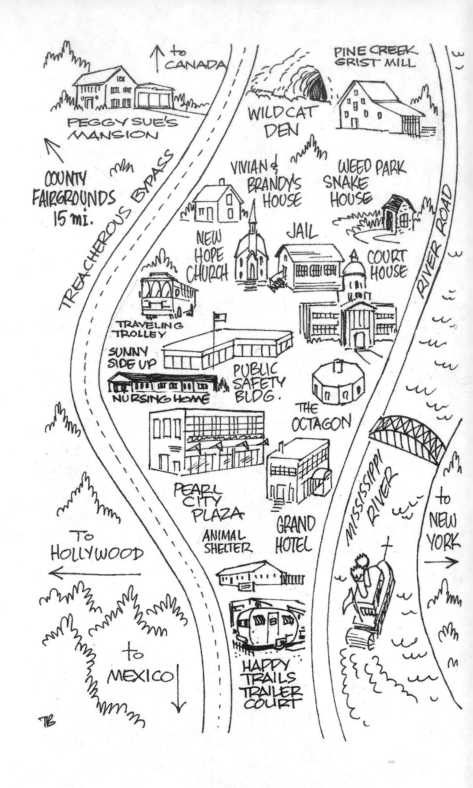

CHAPTER ONE:
MARKET IN THE
BOOK

The snow had begun falling in the late afternoon — big, wet flakes that stuck to the rooftops of houses like dollops of marshmallow cream, and coated bare branches with hardened white chocolate, and covered the ground in fluffy cotton candy. (I've been off sugar for a while and it's just *killing* me.)

I was sitting in the living room on a needlepoint Queen Anne armchair, gazing out the front picture window at the wintry wonderland, waiting for Mother to come downstairs. Sushi, my brown and white shih tzu, lounged on my lap, facing the window, too — but she couldn't see anything because the diabetes had taken away her vision.

Soosh, however, seemed content, and any impartial observer who hadn't caught sight of the doggie's milky-white orbs would swear she was taking it all in. I imagine she could still picture what was going on outside, her ears perking every now and again at the muffled rumble of a snow plow, or the scrape, scrape, scraping of a metal shovel along the sidewalk. (Mr. Fusselman, who lived across the street in a brick Dutch Colonial, had been coming out of his house every half hour to keep the pesky snow off his front walk; I, no fool — at least where shoveling was concerned — wasn't about to tackle ours until the very last flake had fallen.)

I sighed and gazed at the Christmas tree that was in its usual spot next to the fireplace. The fake tree, with fake white tipping (which made Sushi sneeze), had been up since early November, as Mother jumps the gun on everything. (Christmas cards go out in October.) She still decorated the tree with things I had made since the first grade, and many were falling apart, like the clay Baby Jesus that had lost its legs (makes walking on water way tougher). But mostly, hanging from the branches by green velvet ribbons, were small antique items, like red plastic cookie cutters, Victorian silver spoons, floral china teacups, and colorful Bakelite jewelry. One year, however, when I was in middle school, Mother went overboard with her antiques decorating and jammed an old sled in the middle of the tree, and it fell over, knocking our one-eyed parrot off its perch.

For those just joining in (where have you been?), I'll lay in some backstory — all others (unless in need of a refresher course) may feel free to skip ahead to the paragraph beginning, "I stood, giving my butt cheeks a break," etc.

My name is Brandy Borne. I'm a blue-eyed, bottle-blond, thirty-one-year-old, Prozac-prescribed recent divorcée who has moved back to her small, Midwestern Mississippi River hometown of Serenity to live with my widowed mother, who is bipolar. Mother, a spry seventy-four — she claims she's seventy and from here on probably always will — spends her time hunting for antiques, acting in community theater, and reading mysteries with her "Red-Hatted League" gal-pals. Roger, my ex (early forties), has custody of Jake (age eleven), and they live in a beautiful home in an upscale suburb of Chicago, an idyllic existence that I forfeited due to doing something really stupid at my ten-year class reunion two years ago (involving an old boyfriend, alcohol, a condom, and poor judgment).

I have one sibling, an older sister named Peggy Sue, who lives with her family in a tonier part of town; but Sis and I have an uneasy relationship, due to the span of our ages (nineteen years) and difference in politics, temperaments, and lifestyles — not to mention clothing styles (hers, high fashion; mine, low prices). Therefore, a truce is the best we can hope for. Peggy Sue, by the way, is still ragging me for not getting a good settlement out of my busted marriage, but everything Roger and I had — which was substantial — had been earned by his brain and sweat, and I just couldn't ask for what wasn't mine. I do have *some* scruples, even if they didn't extend to ten-year class reunions. . . .

I stood, giving my butt cheeks a break from the uncomfortable antique chair, and replaced Sushi on the hard cushion — she jumped down, not liking it, either — and then I wandered into the library/music room to check on my latest painting.

Was I, perhaps, an artist? Someone who toiled in oil on canvas, waiting for her genius to be discovered? Hardly. Unless you count covering the bottom soles of an inexpensive pair of black high heels in red lacquer to make them look like expensive Christian Louboutin's. (I don't know why I bothered; inside, I'd always know they were a cheat.)

I picked up a shoe to see if it was dry, and

left a fingerprint in the still-gooey paint. (Sigh.)

Mother, who also had a painting project in progress on the plastic-protected library table, was having more success. She had taken the little dead bonsai tree I had given her during her last bout with depression (I didn't *give* it to her dead — she forgot to water it) and had resurrected the tiny tree (or entombed it?) by covering the brown branches with green spray paint. Brilliant!

I returned to the living room to see what was keeping Mother. We had preshow tickets this evening to the winter flea market event, and should have left a half hour ago for the county fairgrounds.

Mother and I maintained a booth at an antiques mall downtown and desperately needed to restock it with new merchandise for the holiday season. We also desperately needed to make a buck or two, since she was on a fixed income, and I wasn't working. (Okay, I did receive alimony — *that* many scruples I haven't.)

I crossed to the banister and gazed upstairs, where a good deal of banging and thumping had been going on.

"What are you doing up there?" I hollered.

Mother's muffled voice came back. "Be down in a minute, dear — keep your little drawers on!"

In Mother's eyes I was perpetually five. I guess if she could be perpetually seventy, I could be perpetually a kindergartner.

So I stood and waited, because there is no other choice with a diva, and in another minute Vivian Borne herself descended, wearing her favorite emerald-green velour slacks and top. Coming straight down would have lacked drama, however, and Mother halted on the landing and, with hands on hips, cast me an accusatory glare through thick-lensed glasses that magnified her eyes to owlish dimensions.

"*Where,*" she demanded regally, "is my raccoon coat?"

The hairs on the back of my neck began to tingle. I narrowed my eyes. When in doubt, answer a question with a question: "Why?"

"*Why?* Because I want to wear it, that's why! What have you *done* with it?"

This was not as unreasonable a question as you might suspect. I had been known to take certain measures with that particular garment.

Displaying the confidence and grace of a child with a chocolate-smeared face being asked about the whereabouts of a missing cake, I said, "I . . . I, uh, I put it in the at-

14

tic . . . in the trunk. . . ."

"What? *Why?*"

"To store it," I said lamely.

Mother sighed disagreeably. "Dear, you know I like to keep that coat in my closet where I can get to it. It's my favorite!" She turned on her heels and marched back up the stairs.

I shivered.

You would, too, if you'd spent your formative years in that house with that woman. Nothing could strike more terror in little Brandy's heart than the sight of her mother in that raccoon coat.

I don't know when Mother had bought it . . . probably in the 1940s (judging by the severe shoulder pads) when she was in college and Father was off being a war correspondent in Germany. I'd always pictured Mother wearing the raccoon coat while riding around in an open jalopy with ten other kids, waving a school banner and shouting "Boola-boola" into a megaphone, like in an old Andy Hardy movie. (Not that there are any new Andy Hardy movies out there.)

But over the years, the coat — besides keeping moths fat and harvesting bald patches — had taken on a more disturbing significance than just the benign symbol of

15

the bobbysoxed, jitterbugging Mother who once walked the earth with other hepcat dinosaurs. From the dawn of Brandy, that coat had been the magic armor Mother always insisted upon donning at the beginning of her manic phase (this included summer!).

Once, during my teen years, after Mother got better, I threw the coat out with the trash . . . then retrieved it before the garbage truck came around. After all, I reasoned, what better early warning system was there to alert me of her deteriorating condition?

And so, perhaps you now have a small understanding of just how worried I was at this moment. If not, let's just say if we were on a submarine, a horn would be blaring *ah-OOO-guh! ah-OOO-guh!* and Brandy would be yelling, "Dive! Dive! *Dive!*"

So when Mother tromped back down the stairs wearing the full-length ratty raccoon coat, I hadn't moved from my frozen spot by the banister. Again, she paused on the landing, this time to look at me intently.

"Brandy, darling, if you're worried about my mental health, you needn't be," she said. "I am quite current on my medication."

"I . . . ah . . . er . . . ah. . . ."

And, having said my piece, I shut my mouth.

Mother was frowning thoughtfully and raising a theatrical finger. "We can't look like we have any *money,* dear. You know how some of those dealers are at a major flea market like this one! They'll send the price sky-high if they think we're women of means."

I nodded, sighing inwardly with relief.

An eyebrow arched, Mother was studying my designer jeans and cashmere turtleneck. "What are you going to wear, dear? I mean, which coat? I suppose they won't see what we have on underneath. . . ."

I said, "I only have my black wool."

Mother made a scoffing sound. "Far too good . . . I'll find something for you in the front closet."

Which was better than something from the attic.

While Mother rooted around raccoonlike in the entryway, I took the time to put Sushi out again. Diabetic animals have to pee a lot because they drink so much, and Soosh was no exception. The nice thing about winter is that she can't stand the cold, and when she does her business, she's quick about it — no sniffing each and every blade of grass, or checking to see if any other animal had dared trespass and soil her sacred ground.

I returned to find raccoon-coated Mother holding aloft a sad-looking, strangely stained trench coat, which I dutifully put on so we could get the heck out of there.

As we exited out the front door into the chill air, I suggested, "Let's take your car. It hasn't been driven in a while."

Mother had an old pea-green Audi that was stored in a stand-alone garage. "Stored" because she lost her license to drive it. Several times, however, she had used it for "emergencies" — once to help me[*] and again to help her grandson, Jake[**] — which caused her suspended license to become a revoked license.

I turned the key in the ignition and the Audi whined. How dare we wake it from its deep slumber on such a cold winter night? The car shuddered and shook and wheezed and coughed, but I forced it to life, and we backed out of the garage and into the street. I turned the Audi toward the bypass, which would lead us to a blacktop road that would then take us to the fairgrounds.

Five minutes into the trip, I sniffed the air and asked, "What smells?"

Mother was studying the winter landscape

[*]*Antiques Roadkill*
[**]*Antiques Maul*

gliding past her mostly fogged-up window a little too intently. "Pardon?"

"What . . . *stinks?*"

Overly casual, Mother replied, "Oh . . . that would be the hamburger grease."

"Hamburger grease."

"Yes, dear. Hamburger grease."

"*What* hamburger grease?"

She was pretending to be enthralled by the vista barely visible out her frosted view on the world. "Why, the hamburger grease I smeared on your coat."

"*What!*"

"It looked far too pristine, dear — I told you, we mustn't appear as if we have much money."

"Well, we *don't* have much money!" I snapped, then grumbled, "Great. Now I look poor *and* smell. I love it when a plan comes together." I powered down both front windows to get rid of the odor.

"Brandy!" Mother protested. "I'm *cold.*"

"Good! I hope you catch one."

For the next ten minutes, all that could be heard was the howling wind blowing in from my window (Mother had rolled hers up) and the castanet chattering of our teeth. But before icicles had a chance to form on the end of our noses, in that jaunty Jack Frost fashion, the bright lights from the county fairgrounds could be seen, and I wheeled off the highway and into the snowy drive leading up to the main building. As I slowed to a stop in front of the large, one-story, maintenance-type structure, Mother hopped out like a hobo from a train and I proceeded on to find a parking spot in the already filled lot.

Man may be able to fly to the moon, clone animals, create bionic body parts, and keep his balance while exercising on a Body Dome. But he (or she) remains powerless to park in a straight row once the snow has obliterated the lines.

After dead-ending down two different lanes, I gave up and added to the confusion, inventing a spot along a far fence.

The temperature had dropped, and my breath mocked me by making smoke worthy of the warmest fire. Hunkered over, I trudged through the white toward the welcoming lights of the building, big wet flakes clinging to my hair and shoulders like the dandruff of a giant.

Just a few hundred feet away from the sanctuary of the building, however, I heard a long, low growl behind me. Then another. And another.

I turned.

Darting out from a row of parked cars

came a pack of wild dogs. They were heading straight for me and didn't seem friendly, so I began to run (well, first I went, "Yikes!"), but the snow — nearly four inches deep now — impeded my flight, and even though the front door to the building seemed close, I knew I couldn't make it before the dogs were on me.

I tore off my coat as the lead dog — a black mongrel apparently pissed for being passed over for the movie version of *Cujo* — snapped at my heels. Then I whirled, throwing the garment on top of him, and made my final dash toward the building. Reaching the door, I risked a glance over my shoulder. The pack, five in all, were tearing my trench coat to pieces!

What if I'd still been inside the thing?

As I stepped into the safety of the building, shivering with more than the chill, it finally dawned on me that the *coat* was what the dogs had been after — drawn by the smell of the hamburger grease.

And the scoreboard reads: Mother, one; Brandy, zero.

The flea market preshow was in full swing, and I was a little surprised by the good quality of the merchandise — these were some high-class fleas! (I'd been to some where I really had gone home with fleas.)

There were at least one hundred dealers hawking their wares — furniture, china, pottery, vintage clothes, jewelry, books, toys, and assorted collectibles. The sight was dizzying, the sounds deafening, as a sea of winter-clad shoppers scurried about, trying to beat the other guy out of an early bargain.

I took a moment to gather my thoughts. Before we'd left home, Mother and I had devised a game plan and divvied up the money. Since she was the expert on glassware — that is to say, more expert than me (which isn't saying much) — Mother was to look for such items. I, on the other hand, had more knowledge about collectibles (which also isn't saying much) and was to cover that ground.

And because our booth already had enough furniture to sell, we agreed to ignore anything along those lines, particularly if bulky — unless the item was a steal, of course.

Antiques dealers — like all store retailers — depend on good pre-Christmas sales in order to make money. It can mean the difference between dealers keeping their heads above water for the entire year, or going under. But trying to figure out what tickles the public's fancy around Christmastime is difficult; buy the wrong thing, and not only has a dealer laid out good money, he's stuck with the item.

But before jumping into the frenzy and fray, I first had to find a new coat . . . because, in spite of the number of people in the building, it was freezing inside! I doubted there was any heat going at all.

I zeroed in on a table of women's fur coats that shared space with a collection of Annalee Christmas dolls, and seeing so many of the Elves and Mice and Santas grouped together with their demented expressions was decidedly unsettling.

I pointed to the fur coats that were piled on top of each other like a bunch of sleeping critters, and asked the middle-aged lady attending the zoo, "How much?"

She studied me through her outdated, oversized round glasses, the bottom halves of which were tinted a pale pink so she didn't have to wear blush (who came up with *that* dumb idea?).

"Twenty-five dollars each," she said.

I showed disappointment in my face.

She held her ground.

I stood mine.

Then she must have taken pity on me — anyway, on my dripping wet hair and shivering body — because the woman said, "I . . . I do have one other fur that I didn't put out because I'm sure it wouldn't sell. . . ."

"How much?"

"Oh, you can have it."

I brightened. "I'll take it! Whatever it is. . . ."

The lady bent and rummaged under the table and then dragged out the freebie: a ratty raccoon coat, bald-patched, moth-eaten, and nearly identical to Mother's.

I reached for my karma gratefully and thanked her.

It wasn't until two hours later that I finally crossed paths with Mother. She was standing by a table of old toys and memorabilia, multiple bags of her flea market finds dangling from each arm while she chatted with a pudgy middle-aged man wearing a plaid coat.

As I approached, it became clear, however, that their exchange was more confrontational than conversational.

Mother was saying, "That book of Mr. Yeager's is worth *far* more than one hundred dollars! That's a famous title and it's a first edition. Clearly, he didn't know what he had, and you are simply out to take advantage of him."

Mr. Yeager, I deduced, was the elderly frail-looking gentleman in a black parka, seated behind the table, and looking increasingly uncomfortable at the unfolding drama. On stage and off, Mother was famous for creating memorable scenes.

Pudgy tightened his grip on the item in dispute — a hardcover book that said *Tarzan of the Apes* on its dust jacket, and featured its branch-swinging hero in silhouette.

"It's marked one hundred dollars," he snapped at Mother, "and that's what I'm going to pay for it!" Then he looked pointedly at Mr. Yeager, saying, "There *are* certain rules that dealers have to abide, you know."

I butted in. "Just a moment . . . has Mr. Yeager accepted any money yet?"

Mother turned to see me, gave my raccoon coat a double take, but wasn't thrown enough to stop her performance. (Once, when Mother was doing *The Vagina Monologues,* some unfortunate woman in the front row was so rude as to have a heart attack and keel over, and the paramedics came, performed CPR, then carried the revived lady out of the theater on a stretcher, while Mother never missed a line.)

"My daughter has a point," Mother snapped back at Pudgy. "The transaction has not yet been completed, and therefore can be taken off the table, so to speak, *if* the dealer wishes it."

All eyes turned to the elderly Mr. Yeager, who said in a frail voice, "I . . . I . . . *do* want to withdraw the book."

"Well!" huffed Pudgy, his fat fingers still clutching the object of his desire. "This is quite unheard of, and I feel compelled to report your conduct, sir, to the organizers of this flea market."

Now might be a good time to mention that Mr. Yeager had a helper seated beside him behind the table. She was about twenty, wearing all black, which extended from her jeans and leather jacket to her short, spiky hair. Her elfin features were not unattractive, though certainly not helped by multiple piercing (ears, eyebrows, nose) and a tattoo of barbed wire that encircled her neck.

At the threat of discrediting the old man, Goth Girl bolted out of her folding chair and flew around the table to face Pudgy.

"Oy!" she shouted in a thick Brit accent, her dark tinted lips peeled back revealing the metal grillwork on her front teeth. "You 'eard me grandad! 'E don't wanna sell it!"

And she snatched the book out of Pudgy's hands.

Pudgy's mouth dropped open, closed, then opened again. "I . . . I'm going to report you *both!*"

Goth Girl, who was a good foot shorter than the portly man, shouted up into his red face, "That's a load of bollocks, you dodgy ol' punter! Now *piss* off!"

Pudgy backed away, turned, and fled, pushing his way through a number of folks who had gathered in the aisle drawn by the impromptu skit.

Impressed by Goth Girl's moxie, I stuck out my hand. "Hi. My name's Brandy."

She extended one black nailed hand. "Chaz."

Mother beamed royally at the young woman, and said, "And I'm Vivian, my dear, Brandy's mother. You handle yourself *quite* well. . . . Have you ever heeded the siren song of the footlights?"

Chaz screwed up her face. "Put me foot *where?*"

"Theater," Mother explained, pronouncing it *thee*-ah-tah. "I'm the current director of the Playhouse and wish to know if you've ever acted."

"Oh, yeah, sure," Chaz nodded. "This one time, I did the Artful Dodger at Holloway's, innit?"

Mother frowned curiously. "Holloway's? I'm not familiar with that theater. . . . Is it in the West End?"

"Naw," Chaz said, "Islington." She made

a face like she'd sucked on a lemon. "Place is a pile of piss, man . . . full of rats and cockroaches."

Mother gave a short laugh. "Well, many of the older buildings are like that . . . but still, they do have their charm."

Chaz made the face again. "Eh? Wha' you on about?"

I intervened. "I believe Holloway is a women's prison, Mother — isn't that right, Chaz?" It pays to watch BBC America.

Chaz smiled, showing the metal grillwork. "That's right, Bran. . . . Mind if I call you that, luv?"

Chaz didn't wait for my reply before going on. "Anyway, when I got outta that dump, I come straight to the States to find me granddad, yeah?" She beamed back at Mr. Yeager, who had remained seated behind the table.

Mr. Yeager nodded, smiling shyly. "That was three months ago," the old gent said softly, "and Chaz has been living with me ever since."

The gawkers had moved on, now that the conflict had ended, except for a man Mother's age named Ivan Wright, who had once been mayor of Serenity, and was among the many old boys in town who Mother was convinced had the hots for her — or anyway, the warms.

Ivan interjected himself into the conversation. "Wasn't that quite a shock, Walter?" the ex-mayor asked Mr. Yeager, his friendly tone taking the edge off his words. "I mean, having this young lady show up on your doorstep claiming to be your granddaughter? How did that happen, exactly?"

Chaz, annoyed by the intrusion — and perhaps the negative content of what Ivan said — snapped, "Well, 'e shagged me grandmum *exac'ly,* didn't 'e? That's 'ow it 'appened, innit?"

I stifled a smile. Mother didn't, letting a grin blossom; she had something like admiration in her big eyes.

"Very succinctly put, my dear," Mother told our new-found friend.

Walter Yeager said proudly, "My granddaughter may be blunt, Ivan, but she's also correct. I met Elsie, her grandmother, when I was stationed in England during the Second World War. After I came back home, she wrote me that we had a son . . . but since I'd married, and Elsie had also found someone, we decided to keep our love child a secret." He paused, then added, "She and I stayed in touch for a while, through the mail . . . but, well, as they say, time marches on. . . ."

Chaz had gone back around the table to stand next to her grandfather; she put one black-nailed hand on his slight shoulder. "I located Granddad from some old letters in a trunk, yeah?"

Yeager looked up adoringly at the girl. "Now that my wife has passed on," he said, "I'm thankful Chaz and I — a couple of lost souls — have found each other." He gave her arm a squeeze. "And I'm relieved that the secret I've carried with me for so many years is finally out."

Ivan smirked, just a bit. "Well, in your case it worked out, but sometimes secrets are best kept secrets . . . especially when nothing good can come of it."

The remark reminded me of something that had been troubling me for weeks on end, thanks to an anonymous letter that had questioned my own parentage. I sneaked a glance at Mother. *Was she keeping a secret from me?* But her face looked placid, even serene.

Walter shook his head. "I used to think that way, Ivan . . . but not anymore . . . not since this little bundle from Britain appeared on my doorstep. Now I want to make it up to her, give her things I couldn't before . . . and that takes money. That's why I'm selling all my old collectibles — memories, if you will."

Ivan's smirk morphed into a smile. "Well, hell, I'll buy this Hopalong Cassidy coffee mug, Walter . . . if that will help. A friend of mine has a son who grew up on Hoppy who'll get a kick out of this."

Yeager smiled. "It's a start. . . ."

The ex-mayor brought out his wallet, but the transaction was interrupted by a commotion nearby, punctuated by shouts of *"Thief!"* and *"Stop him!"*

Sprinting toward me came a young man in torn jeans, a navy sweatshirt, and with a stocking cap pulled down low to right above wild wide eyes. While everyone else jumped out of the young man's way, I positioned myself so I could, at just the right moment, stick out my foot and trip him.

But the second I lifted my leg, Chaz whispered out sharply, "Bran!" and I hesitated just long enough to miss my chance.

The thief whisked by, shoving patrons out of his way, some clearing the path on their own volition — and no other would-be heroes (or heroines, either) risked tripping the kid or tackling him or otherwise keeping him from bolting out the front door. Which he did.

I frowned at Chaz, more in confusion than irritation.

31

She shrugged. "Sorry, Bran . . . thought 'e might 'urt you, mate."

Or that I might hurt *him?*

In short order, the floor manager had called the police, and in less than ten minutes, a uniformed officer arrived. I wasn't surprised that the representative of Serenity's finest who answered the call was none other than my boyfriend, Brian Lawson, who worked the Serenity PD night shift.

As soon as Brian stepped inside, he spotted me and Mother, and shook his head as he approached us down the aisle.

"I might have known," he said with a tiny, wry smile forming on that handsome mug. "If the Borne girls aren't in the middle of trouble, they're bound to be somewhere on the fringes. . . ."

Among those who stood shivering in the blast of cold air that had come in with Officer Lawson were Chaz and the dealer who had been robbed — a gray-bearded, potbellied guy in a plaid shirt and jeans who ran a local antiques shop. Mr. Yeager remained back at his table, and Ivan had moved along.

Brian asked our group, "Who's making the complaint?"

"Complaint, my foot!" the dealer fumed. "I want to make a charge! And I want you to actually *do* something about it!"

Complaint, his foot? Funny he should say that, because I'd never seen this guy on his feet before. Whenever you entered his shop, he was sitting in a rocker, reading a newspaper and letting his wife handle the customers. I figured he was more irritated about having to exert himself than getting robbed.

"All right, settle down," Brian said, not unkindly, patting the air with a hand, "I'm here to help." He withdrew a small tape recorder from his jacket pocket. "Let's start with your name, and then tell me what happened."

The dealer took a deep breath. "I'm Claude Anderson and I have one of the dealers' tables over there . . ." He pointed. ". . . and I'd just turned my back for a second when that punk stole my money!"

Brian asked, "He came around behind the table?"

"Yes! I had the money in a plastic zipper bag — you know, like the bank gives you. . . ."

"And where was the bag?"

"On the seat of my folding chair. I'd gotten up to make change for a customer . . ."

Wow, the guy was going all out all tonight.

". . . and then put the bag down on it

while I wrapped the purchase . . . and the next thing I know this thief is running off with it."

"Can you describe him?"

Anderson said in frustration, "I only saw the back of him!" He pointed an accusatory finger at me — apparently the front of my face resembled the back of the thief's head. "But that girl must've gotten a good look! He ran right past her!"

I started to say something, but shut my mouth because Chaz had moved close to me and surreptitiously took hold of my hand at my side and squeezed it. Hard.

Brian looked at me. "Well?"

"I really didn't get *that* good a look," I said. "He went by so fast — dark jeans, sweatshirt, stocking cap — that's all I remember."

Brian asked Chaz. "How about you?"

Chaz made an exaggerated frown and shook her head. "Seen one bloke you seen 'em all, innit?"

He turned to Mother. "What about you, Mrs. Borne? You're generally observant."

Mother gestured to her thick glasses, "Oh, well, I appreciate the compliment, Officer Lawson . . . but honestly, I didn't see a thing . . . not with *these* poor old peepers."

Brian sighed, hit the stop button on the

recorder.

Mother added, "However, I do have one important question. . . ."

Officer Lawson raised his eyebrows. "Which is?"

"Is there any truth to the rumor that you're going to stop using the ten-codes like some other police departments?"

Brian gaped at Mother at this non sequitur; I stifled a groan and faded back behind Chaz.

"No, Mrs. Borne, we haven't dispensed with them yet."

"Good," Mother said approvingly, tossing her head back. "It's a most efficient system — if it ain't broke, don't fix it!"

Why did Mother care? Because Vivian Borne had her very own code number unofficially assigned by the Serenity PD; when the police radioed "ten-one-hundred" it meant that Mother was on the scene and to proceed with extreme caution.

Anderson said irritably, "Look, can we get back to my stolen money?"

Brian nodded, and told our little group, "All right, you can all go except for Mr. Anderson." Then he took the dealer by the arm and walked him over to his table to finish the interview, leaving Mother, me, and Chaz.

Mother said to me cheerily, "Well, wasn't that exciting? We haven't been involved with a crime for *months!*"

"We're *not* involved."

"We're witnesses, aren't we?" She leaned close and whispered theatrically: "Incidentally, why are we covering up, dear?"

"What?"

"Why aren't we telling your nice young officer what we saw? I was simply following your lead, dear."

"Follow this lead," I said, and made a "zip" gesture across my mouth.

I told Mother to wait while I went to fetch the car, then turned to Chaz with a forced smile. "Can I see you outside for a moment?"

She swallowed and nodded and we stepped out into the cold and stood under the scant protection of the tin awning, our breaths pluming.

Chaz spoke first. "Thanks for keeping your gob shut, Bran, and not grassing."

I said testily, "I know you're involved somehow in that theft."

"Wha'? No way, man!"

I ignored her. "And if you don't want me to 'grass,' that money better be returned to me tomorrow, or I'm gonna suddenly remember all kinds of details about that boy, and no doubt so will Mother — including the spider tattoo on the side of his neck."

Chaz spat, "Bloody hell! I told 'im to cover up that bugger!" She sighed resignedly. "You win, mate. I'll make 'im give back the money. He just did it for me because —"

"I don't want to know," I snapped. "I've already lied once to my boyfriend, and I don't want to do it again."

Her eyes widened. "That screw's your bloke?"

That sounded backward somehow.

But I said, "That's right . . . so you know I mean business, 'mate.' I'll come to your house tomorrow, around noon, and you'd better have that cash — every bleeding quid! Where do you live?"

"Grandad 'as a caravan at Happy Trails Trailer Court . . . Number 21. But I don't want me grandad to know!"

"Don't worry . . . I'll bring some information on the value of that Tarzan book along, as an excuse."

"Okay." She cast her eyes downward. "Thanks, luv."

"Why don't you find some nice friends?"

Chaz looked up again. "Wha'? A ex-con with a funny accent like me? Who's gonna wanna be mates with me?"

"Well . . . me, for one. *If* that money's

returned . . . and if you stay out of trouble, Chaz."

"A posh lady like you?"

I snorted. "I'm not posh. Far from it. Take a closer look at this raccoon coat." We were both shivering, so I said, "Remember, Chaz . . . noon tomorrow."

She said, "I won't let you down," and her smile had a shyness at odds with the spiky hair, multiple piercings, and public theft.

She slipped inside.

I trudged into the snow to get the car, wondering if I'd done the right thing.

On the drive home Mother was a chatterbox, carrying on about her fabulous finds, interspersed with melodramatic rambling about poor Walter Yeager having to sell all his childhood memories. I concentrated on keeping the car on the snowy road, grunting every now and then to show I was listening, even though I wasn't, really.

As we pulled the Audi into the garage, Mother suddenly asked, "Why did you cover up for Chaz, dear?"

I'd hoped we wouldn't be returning to this subject, that I'd ignored her sufficiently to put it out of her mind. Out of her mind was right.

Mother sighed. "Well, I'm sure you have your reasons, and you know I'm never one to pry. . . . By the way, where did you get that wonderful coat? We could be twins."

I shut off the engine and smiled nastily. "Yes, Mother, I feel like your twin. . . . And from now on, whenever I wear this coat, you should be afraid . . . you should be very, very afraid."

Mother frowned and opened her car door. "I don't know what's gotten into you lately, Brandy . . . but I'm glad we're both seeing our therapists tomorrow."

"Me, too," I said, meaning it.

Because Mother was keeping something from me that was way more important than withholding a little information from the police.

And Mother had been keeping her secret a whole lot longer.

A TRASH 'N' TREASURES TIP

Shopping can be daunting at a flea market, where treasures are often hidden among the trash — like the rare photo of Edgar Allan Poe some lucky buyer purchased for a pittance and then sold for thirty-five thousand. Bet that dealer's kicking himself. So am I — I passed it up!

CHAPTER TWO:
SLAY BELLS RING,
ARE YOU LISTENING?

The next morning, Mother and I had same-time appointments at the mental health clinic with our respective doctors (hers, a psychiatrist; mine, a psychologist), and at a little before ten, I pulled my new used burgundy Buick into the snow-plowed parking lot. I had recently bought the "gently dented" car from Mrs. Hetzler — a friend of Mother's in her Red-Hatted League mystery-reading club — who had shrunk so much over the years that the little woman could no longer see over the steering wheel without sitting on a Chicago phone book.

Whenever I enter the waiting room of the clinic and see all of the other patients in need of mental care, I'm reminded of a story Pastor Tutor shared in a sermon one Sunday — you know how it goes . . . about the room filled with looming crosses to bear, and you go, "I'll take that little one over there." And God goes, "That's the one you came in with." And you go, "Oh."

After stomping the white stuff from our boots, Mother and I checked in with the receptionist, then hung up our twin raccoon coats. (I continued to wear mine, whether out of defiance or despair, I'll leave for you to judge.) Then I found a chair among the other tortured seated souls, and went about selecting a dog-eared magazine from the mundane reading material (nothing too depressing, of course) scattered on a nearby end table. I chose *Highlights* — never saw much in Gallant, always carrying a secret torch for Goofus.

Mother, however, refused to light, flitting from one person to the next to inquire how he/she was doing, knowing not only their names, but each person's mental condition and what medications they were currently taking, right down to asking with dramatic concern about the various side effects of those meds as based upon what she'd heard listed on television commercials.

Halfway through a *Highlights* story about an older and younger sister who put aside their problems to help their folks out around the house (science fiction for kids), my attention was diverted to the familiar figure of a tall, lanky, sandy-haired guy who was walking toward me from the psychiatrist's wing.

Seeing me, Joe Lange lit up like Christmas lights, and I flashed him a big smile. We had been friends ever since community college when we'd been thrown together as partners in biology lab, where I'd had to either learn to like the irritating, know-it-all nerd, or filet him with my frog-dissecting knife.

"Hi, Brandy," Joe said with his shy grin, planting himself in front of my chair like a palm tree. He was wearing brown corduroy slacks and a burgundy-and-gold stripped rugby shirt, which was a change from his summer attire of army fatigues. That time of year, his hair was short-cropped, not his current unruly haystack.

Allow me to explain. During college, Joe Lange — a pop-culture junkie raised on John Wayne and Superman and other macho fantasies — had joined the National Guard with the idea of playing military on the weekends, which during peacetime sounded like fun.

Then came Desert Storm.

And Joe, along with thousands of other National Guards-men (and -women), suddenly got called into real combat and found out firsthand what war was all about. After a harrowing battle — involving a blinding sandstorm that led to heavy casualties from friendly fire — my lab partner got sent home for combat stress reaction (known in days gone by as battle fatigue and shell shock).

While Joe has never been what you'd call fully recovered, I considered him *nearly* normal and certainly harmless, *if* he stayed on his meds — as he apparently was now. Otherwise, my old pal would become a one-man commando unit — albeit a harmless one — who spent his days patrolling the woods of Wild Cat Den State Park, protecting the unsuspecting, visiting public from imagined terrorist incursion.

I patted the just-vacated seat next to me. "Join me. Good to see you back in civies."

Joe slid into the chair. "I don't go out to the park during the winter, you know."

It was also hard to get used to Joe talking like a normal person and not a walking army-lingo lexicon, which usually left *me* in "zero-dark-thirty."

"Yeah," I said, "bet it gets kinda cold in those caves, unless you got a bear-size fur coat."

"The bears out there have them already."

"Right. *Are* there bears out there?" I asked.

"You bet. Wildcats, too. That's why they call it Wild Cat Den."

"Is that right? You learn something every day."

Joe shifted to look at me; his features were nice enough, but everything seemed a bit askew — one eye a little higher than the other, mouth a tad wide, nose leaning a bit to one side. "Saw you at the flea market last night."

"You were there, too? You should have said hi."

I knew Joe collected televison and movie memorabilia, like *Star Trek* and *Star Wars*. He even wrote articles online, including one that made a compelling if nonsensical case that the science-fiction show *Firefly* had named its crew's spacecraft *Serenity* after his hometown.

"I went early, but left after a while." He shrugged. "Nothing but the same old junk. You know how flea markets are."

"Oh, I don't know," I countered. "Mr. Yeager had a first edition of the original Tarzan novel for a measly hundred bucks."

Joe popped up like burnt bread in a toaster. "You're kidding me! Are you *serious?* Who got it? *You?*"

I raised a calming palm. "Whoa, Big Fella. Nobody got it. But somebody almost got *took*."

And I relayed the tale of the altercation

that had taken place between Mother and the pudgy book scout who'd tried to take advantage of the elderly dealer.

Joe shook his head. "Old Yeager's sure lucky your mom was around." His sigh started at his toes and ended around his scalp. "What I wouldn't give to own that book myself. . . . I only have a beat-up second edition. I'm big into ERB-dom, you know."

To my ears that sounded like a belch followed by "dom." "Into what, Joe?"

"ERB-dom, the fandom of Edgar Rice Burroughs, creator of Tarzan. I have lots of Tarzan books and comics and the Johnny Weissmuller DVD sets, plus John Carter of Mars and the Venus stuff and . . ." Joe's eyes sharpened. "Wonder what Yeager'll ask for it *now*."

I was about to reply that Mother and I were going to see Mr. Yeager after our appointments to discuss that very thing, when the receptionist-behind-the-glass motioned that my doctor was ready to see me.

I bid good-bye to Joe, who had a glassy-eyed, inward expression, then headed down the therapists' wing, arriving at a door marked CYNTHIA HAYS, PH.D., P.C., which I entered without knocking.

The large, rectangular room — its walls

painted a soothing mint green — was divided into two sections. To the left was a homey area where a floral couch and two matching overstuffed chairs huddled around a coffee table on which a pitcher of water and a box of Kleenex awaited the next breakdown. I called this the blubbering section, and so far I'd managed to stay out of it.

To the right was the office area where Dr. Cynthia Hays — wearing clothes as no-nonsense as she was, a beige silk blouse and tailored navy wool slacks — stood next to her desk. She was petite and pretty, with dark blue eyes, a button nose, and a friendly smile. She seemed impossibly young to be a doctor (the woman had to be pushing thirty anyway, but looked about twenty) and my sessions with her were a lot like being lectured by a little sister.

"Hello, Brandy," the therapist said.

" 'Lo, Cynthia." I'd been seeing Dr. Hays long enough that we were on a first-name basis.

I took the patient's chair opposite her. The desk she settled behind was almost comically oversized for the therapist's small frame, but then, who could blame the woman for wanting to put as much distance as possible between herself and her troubled patients?

Cynthia began to review my file, which lay open on the desk in front of her, and as she did, her friendly smile became a frown. I squirmed and pretended to study the various college degrees on the wall behind her, which shared space with a Mary Engelbreit framed poster suggesting, LET'S PUT THE FUN BACK IN DYSFUNCTIONAL.

I could see the truth in that, but I was kind of hoping to put the "functional" back in.

When Cynthia finally looked up at me, concern clouded her eyes. She served up a rumpled smile and said, "I've had several calls about your behavior since our last meeting. . . ."

"From Mother, I suppose."

She nodded. "Yes. But also from other concerned friends."

"Name one."

"How about Tony Cassato?"

"Yeah, how about him?"

So, the Serenity chief of police had made good on his threat of contacting my therapist after I gave Connie Grimes — a venomous gal-pal of my sister Peggy Sue — a gentle shove into a pile of Halloween sweaters at Ingram's department store. (The witch had called Mother and me "crazy," and I don't necessarily disagree, but the grimy Connie still had her nerve.)

I asked indignantly, "Isn't it unethical for you to talk to other people about your patients?"

"I *don't* talk about my patients with other people," Dr. Hays responded patiently, "but I *can* listen. And whether you realize it or not, there *are* people who care enough about you to want to let your doctor know."

I grunted.

Cynthia went on: "Chief Cassato said you were supposed to take an anger management class. . . ."

"Yeah."

"And how did that go?"

"Perfect. It managed to make me angry."

Cynthia didn't find that funny, and studied me with ever-tightening eyes. Then she said quietly, "What is it, Brandy? I thought we were making progress."

I responded by reaching into my black leather Juicy Couture hobo bag that I'd wrestled away from another girl at a half-off sale, and brought out a folded piece of paper, which I slid across her desk. "I got this in the mail a while ago."

Dr. Hays took the paper, opened it, and read the note that said, *Wouldn't you like to know who your real mother is?*

Cynthia slowly set the paper down. "Surely you don't believe this? A cruel note from some crank. . . ."

"Of course I don't," I said coolly, and then burst into tears.

Cynthia came around her desk and, grasping me gently by the elbow, led me over to the blubbering section, where she deposited me on the couch beneath another framed Mary Engelbreit poster that read, SNAP OUT OF IT!

Am I the only one out here who hopes Mary Engelbreit has the occasional really, really lousy day?

Anyway, seated there in Blubber Town, I bawled and wheezed and hacked, and Dr. Hays trotted off, then trotted back and handed me a cup of hot coffee. Apparently, my crying jag called for more than a paltry pitcher of ice water.

Cynthia sat next to me as I delicately sniffled snot. I took a sip of the hot liquid, then said, "Thing is, I *know* it's true!"

"Really?"

"I must've known deep down for a long time, but I just didn't want to admit it . . . didn't even want to *think* about it."

Cynthia said gently, in a tone I imagined she reserved for talking clients down off a ledge, "It's not unusual to feel that the parents who brought you up aren't biologically yours. We often feel apart from our parents, alienated from them; sometimes we even hate them, and we often feel as if we're from some other planet, let alone the same family. Sometimes, Brandy, there's a deep desire within us to be different that can cause a person to fantasize that they were adopted. . . . And sometimes —"

"And sometimes a hot dog is a hot dog, Dr. Freud," I interrupted. "What that letter did was bring everything into focus. You see, I *know* who my real mother is."

Cynthia's left eyebrow rose in a very Mr. Spock-like fashion that no doubt would have impressed Joe Lange.

I finished the thought: "My real mother is my 'sister' — Peggy Sue."

The doctor's eyebrow came down but she said nothing.

"My sister, my mother, my sister, my mother . . . get it? Haven't you ever seen *Chinatown*?"

Cynthia, to her credit after my rude outburst, gave me a tiny smile and a tinier nod. "All right. Let's explore this. What makes you think your sister is your mother?"

"Things," I said with a shrug. "Like the way Peggy Sue has always looked at me with disappointment. Who's ever disappointed in

50

their sister? I mean, you may dislike them, resent them, maybe even hate them . . . but feel disappointment that a sibling hasn't lived up to her potential? That's a *mother* thing!"

She didn't deny it.

"And something else I couldn't put my finger on till now, something else I've seen in her eyes that just doesn't make sense coming from a sister — *regret.*"

Cynthia prodded. "Be specific. Facts, not feelings."

I stared across the room at nothing. "When I was in the hospital last summer, in critical condition, I woke up to hear Peggy Sue saying, 'Brandy . . . I'm sorry . . . I only did what I thought was best.' I didn't know what she was *talking* about . . . but it lingered with me. Then, later, when Mother and I were in a dangerous situation, Mother said to me, 'There's something I have to tell you about Peggy Sue.' After the crisis passed, I asked her what she meant, and Mother denied having said it."

Cynthia asked, "You haven't confronted either your mother or sister about your suspicions?"

I shook my head, reached for a tissue, and dabbed at my eyes. "Mother would lie, of course, to protect Peggy Sue. And Peggy

Sue? Well, that would open a real can of worms for my social-climbing sister."

Cynthia asked, "Do you know who might have sent the note?"

I snorted. "I have one big fat suspect: Connie Grimes. *She's* the reason I had to take that anger management class."

Cynthia gave me a tiny smile. "Well, then, she was just trying to yank your chain with that note, that's all."

I shook my head. "No. It's more than that. Connie *knows* the truth."

"What makes you so sure?"

"Because of the way Peggy Sue behaves around her . . . always kowtowing to that cow's every wish. It's like Sis is *afraid* of her." I took a deep breath, let it out, said woefully, "No, that note rings true, and it points to Peggy Sue."

Suddenly, my sorrow turned to anger, and I set the coffee cup forcefully on the table, spilling it a little.

"And to think!" I said. "Life could have been *so* different for me! *I* could have grown up with *money* and had a *real* sister — Ashley, my niece — and lived *her* kind of privileged life!"

Cynthia cocked her head and countered, "But that's not what would have happened, is it?"

I looked down at my hands in my lap. "No. I suppose not."

"Can you imagine what your life really *would* have been like?"

I looked at her sharply. "I *hate* it when you make me do all the work. Is *that* what you get paid the big bucks for?"

"Sometimes, yes," Cynthia said, then waited patiently.

I sighed. "All right, I'll see if I can come up with a credible scenario. . . . Peggy Sue, knocked up the summer after high school, never goes to college, so she never meets Uncle Bob, who makes all the money that kept Mother and me afloat in the early years. Instead, her boyfriend — my *father,* whoever the hell he is — dumps Sis after finding out she's pregnant, and Peggy Sue has to raise me as a single parent in a time when that was far more taboo, and we live in abject poverty and misery, including Mother, newly widowed and unable to afford mental health care. In desperation, Peggy Sue marries a divorced guy who works at a gas station, and one night he molests me, after I start to blossom. I stab him to death with a kitchen knife, and Peggy Sue covers up the crime by burning down our shack with the body in it. But then she gets caught and, taking the murder rap for

me, goes to jail where she has a lesbian af-
fair with a female guard who —"

"I saw that movie on Lifetime too," Cynthia said caustically.

I shrugged. "Well, at least that little
exercise showed me Peggy Sue *might* have
done the best thing for all of us."

"If you're *right* about this . . ."

"Oh, I'm right!"

". . . then Peggy Sue was just a high school
girl in a terrible situation. You're thinking of
her as the adult Peggy Sue. I'm sure you realize that it was a different time back then,
and much easier to be ostracized. Keep in
mind how hard it would have been, how difficult the choices were."

"Fine, she's a saint, but damn it, she
should have *told* me at some point . . . not
kept it a secret." I smirked. "But then, Sis
always *has* cared more about what *other*
people think than the reality of her life."

Cynthia said, "*You're* accepting your
theory as reality, Brandy. I admit it's credible, but it's just a theory, based on circum-
stantial evidence. You'll never know until
you talk it out with your mother."

"Which one?"

"Peggy Sue."

"Then you *do* think she's my mother!"

We sat in silence for a few moments; then

Cynthia — who had every right to be exasperated with me — said, "I won't tell you what to do, Brandy . . . but if and when you decide to discuss this with your sister, pick a time that you and Peggy Sue can be alone and you can hear her side of the story. Remember, if you're right about this . . . she's been suffering, too." The therapist stood. "I'm sorry, we have to end this now. . . ."

"Jeez, and it was just getting really fun."

Back in the reception room, which was empty now due to the approaching lunch hour, I sat and waited for Mother. I could hear her musical laughter, and the responding laughter from her male psychiatrist, coming from behind the nearest door of the opposite wing. After I cooled my heels for a few more minutes, Mother exited the office, smiling broadly.

"Good news," she exclaimed the moment she'd reached me. "The doctor said that I am no longer bipolar!"

"Really?" I said, amazed, getting to my feet. Was it possible bipolar disorder could leave as quickly as it had come on? That suddenly, one day, a person would wake up and be cured, or anyway in remission?

In Mother's case, I'd have to see some hard evidence.

"Oh, my, yes," Mother rattled on. "And to think, all these years I've been misdiagnosed." Then she crowed in triumph: "I'm actually schizo-affective!"

I raised my eyebrows, "And that's better, how?"

Mother frowned. "Well, doesn't that *sound* more like me?"

I grunted in agreement. Mother certainly was one effective schizoid.

"Remember when we did our musical version of *Three Faces of Eve* at the Playhouse? Now we know why I felt so connected to that role . . . or is it roles?"

I couldn't answer her — I was flashing back to the terror of Mother singing all three parts in the same song, slamming one different hat on after another, like an even more manic Jimmy Durante, to help the audience keep track of the various Eves.

"Schizophrenia isn't multiple personalities, Mother. Your one personality is quite enough." I handed Mother her raccoon coat. "Do you and your doctor *have* to have so much fun?"

Mother appraised me with her eyebrows raised above the magnified eyes behind her oversize thick glasses. "I can see that you're still Little Miss Grumpy Pants. Well, my dear, I don't have to be subjected to your ever-darkening storm clouds cluttering up my perfect blue sky. You can drive me straight back to the house!"

"I thought we were going to see Mr. Yeager," I protested. "To take him the information we found on the internet about his Tarzan book."

(*And* get the money from Chaz that her boyfriend stole.)

Mother harrumphed. "You can go by yourself, Grouchy . . . I'm tired of you raining on my parade!"

Even though Mother's parade was one tuba player, a tractor pulling a hayrack, and a maniacal clown bringing up the rear, I didn't relish driving all the way across town to drop her off.

I gave Mother a smile. "Is this better? I've turned my frown upside down, just for you."

Mother's eyes narrowed to near-normal (magnified) size, and she said skeptically, "It looks a trifle . . . forced."

I smiled wider — dangerously wide for a mental health facility, as certainly somewhere around here a closet filled with coats that buttoned in back were at the ready. "How's *this?*"

"All right, all right, please remove that grotesque grin and we'll go together. . . . But remember, I have no room in my happy world for a Grinch right now."

"Come along with me, Mother, and afterward, we'll watch our *Miracle on 34th Street* DVD and eat microwave popcorn till *we* pop."

Now she was the one with the maniacal grin. "Deal!"

And we trooped out to the car.

Mr. Yeager lived in a trailer court located in a section of town the locals called South End. If Serenity could be said to have a seedier side, this would be it, distinguished by factories belching smoke, a noisy railroad switching yard, a smelly slough, and (as a result) surrounding lower-income housing. In the past few years, however, a concerted effort had been made by the city and its denizens to improve conditions in this part of town, since it was the first impression travelers arriving from the south got of our little burg. Even so, the bleakness of winter — the newly fallen white snow having already turned to black slush — did not help the overall effect.

I drove past a small strip mall, then turned at a convenience store to enter the Happy Trails Trailer Park. Mother predicably began to bray, *"Happy trails to you, until we meet again,"* sounding more like Roy Rogers than Dale Evans, which, in spite of my inner mood, made me laugh. As we headed down the trailer court's main street (paved and plowed), I was pleasantly surprised by what I saw: attractive mobile homes sitting on spacious lots. Christmas lights and decorated trees twinkled in windows and occasional Santa displays and Nativity scenes enlivened the modest yards.

Mr. Yeager lived on Lot Number Twenty-one, and we pulled up in front of his un-Christmas-decorated mobile home, a white, single trailer with a stylish bay-front window. Parked in the drive beneath a white aluminum carport was a tan Ford Taurus that indicated the old gent was home.

Mother and I had just gotten out of our car when I spotted Chaz down the street a ways, walking briskly toward us. She was dressed in black again — leather jacket, jeans, motorcycle boots — and when the girl saw us, she waved the stolen zipper bag and yelled for all the world to hear, "*Bran'!* Got the money for ya what me *boyfriend* nicked!"

Mother, next to me, murmured, "So *that's* what this is all about. I do hope you know what you're doing, my dear, aiding and abetting that urchin. . . ."

I walked toward Chaz.

"Wha'?" Chaz frowned as we met in the

street, "You're not 'appy?"

"Yes, I'm happy. But I'll be even happier when this money gets back to its rightful owner."

I held out a hand, and she relinquished the bag.

" 'Ow will you do it?" Chaz asked, her heavily darkened eyebrows knitted. "Don't want me boyfriend to get into trouble, yeah?"

I granted her a smile. "I'll just say I found the bag in the snow when I left the flea market that night."

"Brilliant!" Chaz looked past me. "Where'd your mum go?"

I turned around. Mother had indeed disappeared. I said, "She's probably inside already."

Mother never stood on ceremony; if a door was unlocked, she took it as an open invitation to walk right in.

I put the bank bag in the large tote I was carrying, then followed Chaz up the front steps of the mobile home. The girl was reaching for knob when the door flew open and Mother rushed out, shoving Chaz back into me, and pushing us both down the steps. We didn't fall into the sludgy snow, but it was close.

"*Oy!*" Chaz blurted.

"*Moth*-er," I said crossly. "What's the big idea?"

She raised a palm like an Indian chief in an old movie about to say, "How." "Children . . . you *dear* children . . ."

Chaz and I exchanged "huh" glances.

"I must prepare you," Mother announced. She touched a breast with a hand and gazed skyward in search of just the right words. "Mr. Yaeger is dead as a mackerel."

Chaz shouted, "No *way!*" and, shoving Mother aside, hurried back up the steps and into the trailer.

"*That* was preparing us?" I asked Mother acidly.

She shrugged. "Being direct is always the best approach, I always say. Rip that bandage off! No sense lingering on the unpleasant."

She was right, so I left her unpleasantness behind and went inside, where I found Chaz on her knees in the small kitchen area, leaning over the sprawled-on-his-back, pajama-clad Mr. Walter Yeager. The girl was shaking her grandfather gently, as if he were only in a deep sleep.

Holding up her cell phone as she stood poised in the doorway, Mother said, "I've already called the police."

I put a hand on Chaz's shoulder. "The

paramedics will be here right away."

Mother quipped, "Perhaps not . . . I made it clear the old gent was already dead."

Chaz flew to her feet and pointed a black-nailed forefinger at Mother, shouting, "Me grandad *said* you was a muppet, yeah? Maybe *you* did this to 'im!"

Mother's big eyes blinked behind the big glasses. "Muppet?"

"A *loony* bird, innit?"

I quickly moved between the two. "Mother," I said, "maybe it would be best if you go outside and wait for . . . whoever *is* coming."

Mother frowned at me. "What does she mean by 'a muppet'? Like Kermit or Miss Piggy . . . ?"

"Mother . . . outside. Please." I thought no good would come of explaining to her that a "muppet" meant a crazy person in Brit speak.

Mother nodded. "All right, dear, I'll stand outside and flag down the police car."

"Do that."

Chaz, her cheeks streaked with black mascara, lips trembling, turned to me and asked pitifully, "Can't you do *anything*, Bran?"

I walked over to poor Mr. Yeager; he sure

62

looked like a goner, but I said anyway, "I'll try."

I knelt and went through the motions of chest compressions — like I'd seen done on TV shows — and hoped I wasn't doing the man any more harm. (I had once gone to a mall where CPR classes were being offered, but got distracted by a shoe sale.) Thankfully, before I attempted mouth-to-mouth resuscitation, the sound of a siren reached my ears, and I ceased my useless efforts.

Within another minute, two police officers came through the front door of the trailer. The blue uniform in the lead was Scott Munson, tall and gangly, while on his heels came plainclothes officer Mia Cordona, a dark-haired beauty who had once been a close friend of mine; she was in a black tailored suit, and neither cop wore a topcoat, though both their breaths were pluming in the pre-Christmas chill.

The two officers were well known to Mother and me — and vice versa — and, perhaps understandably, something akin to dread flashed across their faces when they saw us.

Then Munson barked, "Get out of the way!" and Mia corralled us three women in the living room of the trailer, which was separated from the kitchen by a half-wall.

Chaz and I sat on a nubby tan couch, while Mother took a rocker that squeaked. Mia produced a small tape recorder from her coat pocket, and began firing questions.

"And you are . . . ?" Mia asked Chaz.

"Charlotte Doxley. I . . . I'm 'is *gran'daughter*. . . ." Chaz began to sob.

"She came from England a few months ago to live with Mr. Yeager," I offered.

Commotion at the front door halted our interview as the paramedics arrived.

Chaz, her red-swollen eyes darting to the kitchen, started to rise from the couch, but I held her back gently. "Let them do their job. . . . Your grandfather's in good hands, now. . . ."

She swallowed hard and nodded.

Mia pressed on. "Who found the body?"

Mother, rocking in the recliner that squeaked, raised her hand like a student in the back of class and piped up, "That would be *me,* dear."

Mia turned hooded eyes toward Mother. "As briefly as possible, Mrs. Borne. . . ."

Mother, rocking, squeaking, looked shocked. "Why, Mia . . . I'm *always* succinct. I *never* waste words. Brandy, don't I always say, why use two words where one will do? Why give a big speech when a concise statement will suffice? Why —"

64

"That will do *and* it will suffice," Mia snapped, adding, "and would you *stop* that rocking!"

(I was staying out of this, knowing that anyone who tried to limit Mother's verbalizing would be off *their* rocker soon enough.)

Nonetheless, Mother stopped rocking and gave Mia the same kind of appraising look she gave to an antique she was considering for purchase. "Too much caffeine in the morning, my dear? And I see that you're still grinding your teeth." She shook her head, her expression the soul of concern. "Why, when you were a little girl living across the street from us, I thought you might gnash those little choppers down to *stumps. . . .*"

Now I felt I had to come to the aid of my outmatched childhood friend.

"Mother," I said, "Mia is just trying to get the facts straight. You know — like Joe Friday?"

Mother looked at me as if I had spaghetti sauce smeared on my face. "Don't you think I *know* that, dear? And your interrupting is not helping the process. Now where was I? Ah, yes. Brandy and I came to give Walter — Mr. *Yeager* — some information about a valuable book in his possession, and when we arrived, Chaz was walking toward us from up the road."

Chaz interjected, "I was at me mate's last night. Ben Adams, yeah? 'E 'as a caravan up the road."

Mia frowned over her notebook. "A what?"

"Caravan, miss. A . . . what you call it, a *trailer,* yeah?" Then the tears began to flow again. "If I 'adn't been over there with Ben, I woulda been *'ere* for me gran'dad. . . ."

Mother picked the story back up. "While the girls were talking outside the trailer, I went on in — the door being open — and discovered Walter on the floor in the kitchen. I tried to administer CPR but, well, I'm afraid I quickly came to the inevitable conclusion the poor man had been dead for some time."

One of the paramedics entered the living room, and Chaz jumped to her feet. "Me gran'dad?" she asked anxiously.

The paramedic, a young man with a face made old by his job, said, "I'm sorry. There wasn't anything we could do."

Chaz sank back down on the couch and covered her face with her hands.

The paramedic went on: "Based on the medication we found on the kitchen counter, death may have been due to a heart attack . . . but without an autopsy —"

Chaz cried, "No! I won't have me gran'dad cut on!"

Officer Munson had joined us from the kitchen, and he said sympathetically to Chaz, "I understand how you must feel, miss, but the coroner will decide whether or not there will be an autopsy."

Mia looked at Munson. "Has he been called?"

Munson nodded.

I distracted Chaz by putting an arm around her shoulders and asking, "Would you like to stay with us tonight? You really shouldn't be alone."

Chaz shook her head somberly. "Thanks. But I'll go back round to Ben's, yeah?"

Mia, slipping her small tape recorder into a jacket pocket, said, "I'm done with the preliminary interviews, but there may be follow-up. . . . Our condolences, Miss Doxley, on the loss of your grandfather."

Mother rose from the rocker, which made one last squeak. "I assume that at some point someone will be wanting to take our *fingerprints,*" she stated, eyes flaring behind the magnifying glasses.

Everyone stared at her, stupefied. Then Officer Munson asked condescendingly, "And why would we do *that,* Mrs. Borne?"

Mother raised her eyebrows. "Why, to

eliminate us as suspects, of course!"

Mia almost smiled. "Suspects in *what?*"

"The murder of Walter Yeager, of course! Aren't you people *police?*"

A Trash 'n' Treasures Tip

Flea market vendors can be eccentric and difficult, so tread lightly when handling their merchandise, and don't insult them by low-balling their already low prices. If you must bargain, be sly, saying, "What a wonderful item! You have a great eye, sir (ma'am). It's a fair price, just a little out of my price range." That will work — once in a hundred tries.

CHAPTER THREE:
DECK THE MALL

I hardly said three words to Mother on our drive home from Mr. Yeager's. Finding the old gent dead was bad enough, but Mother had outdone herself, upsetting Chaz so much by saying the girl's grandfather was murdered that Officer Munson had yelled at Mother (and me, guilty by association), demanding we leave forthwith, which is police code for get the hell out of here before you cause any more trouble.

Officer Munson had escorted us out to my car — not out of politeness, rather to make sure we left — and I took the opportunity to give the officer the bank bag, instructing him to pass it along to Brian, who would know what to do with it.

Officer Munson had likely been tempted to ask what it was all about, but seemed to know better. His mission was to get rid of us, and he had.

Actually, come to think of it, I did say

three words to Mother on the way home: "You're a troublemaker." To which I got no response, neither dismissive nor indignant. Which was bad — that meant Mother was serious in her belief that Mr. Yeager had been murdered, and the last thing we needed right now was for Vivian to go air-Borne on another amateur sleuthing binge.

At the house, Sushi had piddled in the living room, on the wood floor, fortunately, and not the Persian rug. But the puddle was close enough to the edge of the carpet to send the message that she *could* have peed on the rug *should* she have *wanted* to, and maybe next time she *would* if we ever left her so long again. Remarkable aim for a blind pooch. . . .

I put Soosh out the back door anyway, but she just stood on the frozen stoop with her pug nose in the air and her spooky white eyes turned my way, as if to say, "You're kidding, right?" She made no move to go down the steps, so I brought her back inside.

Then I trooped upstairs to my bedroom, where I found the little devil had dragged a single shoe out of the closet — a Donald Pliner black suede loafer that I'd waited and waited to get further reduced in the sale room of Ingram's, until finally on one hot July day I hunted down the manager of the

70

shoe department and complained, "Come on! These Pliners have been out since last winter! Who else is gonna buy suede loafers in the middle of summer?" And he'd discounted them to seventy-five percent off, out of a sense of fairness.

Or maybe just to get rid of me.

Anyway, the left shoe in the middle of the bedroom was another message from Sushi meant to inform me that she might've turned it into a chew toy with her sharp little teeth and left me with only the right, right? Sushi sure was getting cranky these days . . . but then, being diabetic and blind got a dog cut a lot of slack around the Borne estate.

Returning the shoe to its mate in the closet reminded me that the big sales once held in January were now in December, and Tina — my BFF — and I were due for some serious Christmas shopping. I speed-dialed her on my cell at the Tourism Office downtown, where she worked part-time convincing outsiders to visit our fair city, and we set a date for the next day.

As I left my bedroom, I heard Mother weeping behind her closed bedroom door.

I knocked gently. "Mother . . . are you all right?"

When she didn't respond, I asked, "May I

71

come in?"

There was a muffled sniffle, then a loud, clown-car *honk* as she blew her nose, before she answered, "Yes, dear."

I turned the knob and pushed the door open. Although it was only three in the afternoon, Mother was already in her pink nightgown and under the covers, her head propped up with several pillows. She had a tissue in one hand and was dabbing at her eyes.

I recalled my earlier, caustic remark and said, "I'm sorry I called you a trouble-maker."

Mother sniffled, "That's not why I'm crying, dear. I *know* I'm not a troublemaker."

That made her a majority of one.

I sat on the edge of the bed. "Then what's the matter?"

She heaved a sigh. "I was thinking of Walter."

So that was it.

"Sometimes a shock doesn't hit us until later," I said philosophically, "after a crisis has passed. So it's okay to feel the way you do."

"*That's* not it, dear," Mother replied. "My goodness! Death is an absolute. No one escapes the Grim Reaper. And sadly, some of us, like poor Walter, are fated to depart

72

this world under less than happy circumstances."

"Less than happy circumstances" was an
interesting way to describe being murdered,
if indeed Mr. Yeager *had* been murdered . . .
which I didn't believe was the case.

Mother and I had been involved, or rather
she had gotten us involved, in two murder
mysteries already this year, and another
would strain not just credulity but my sanity. (Mother's sanity didn't enter into it,
since Mother and sanity rarely came up in
the same sentence.)

"No," Mother was saying, "that's not why
I'm crying." She paused dramatically, as if
waiting for me to say my line.

Trouble was, I was still poised patiently in
the wings, only a bit player in Mother's
production.

So Mother pressed on: "I was merely
thinking of my senior high school prom and
how *I* was Walter's *first* that night."

I nodded. "His first prom date, you mean."

Mother shook her head. "No, dear . . . his
first sexual conquest, although I admit to
being rather more cooperative than most
vanquished nations."

I blinked at her a half-dozen times. "You
mean, Walter was *your* first?"

Mother's eyes widened, huge even without

her glasses. "Certainly not! By then I was already quite sexually active. Don't you think you're rather stepping over the line, dear, with these prying questions about something so personal?"

I probably had the expression of somebody slapped with a good-size wet fish. Mother had overloaded my meager mind with TMI (too much information) and somehow simultaneously had placed the blame on my shoulders.

Mother was plowing on. . . .

"You see, many of the boys were going off to war after they graduated that summer — Walter was enlisting in the Army Air Force, who were helping the British RAF fight the Germans bombing England." Mother paused, then said in a hushed voice, as if someone else might be listening, "The dear boy was a virgin, you see, and naturally, I wanted to give him a *nice* send-off."

"Yes, well, I don't really need to —"

"Brandy!" Mother's eyebrows chased her hairline. "What do you mean, taking such a high-and-mighty attitude!"

Me? I didn't recall taking any attitude other than abject shock, but high-and-mighty wasn't it; who was I to judge? I'd been sexually active at her age, too. I just prayed she and I would never discuss it.

74

Mother was saying, "Many of the girls felt as I did . . . old taboos falling away like autumn leaves in wartime. . . . ."

I almost commented to Mother that autumn leaves did not fall in the summer, but I restrained myself.

Her expression had turned thoughtful. "Although, looking back with the wisdom of age, I do have my doubts about our behavior in those days. Oh, not my own! But I'm fairly sure a few of the young men may have taken advantage of their dates that night."

"Date rape? Back then?"

"Boys will be boys."

I wanted to get off this subject ASAP, so I asked, "What happened to you and Mr. Yeager? Were you an item, after that? Were you engaged . . . ?"

"Heavens, no! It was a fling, a mercy —"

"Mother, *please!*"

". . . mission. Anyway, out of sight, out of mind." Mother shrugged pragmatically. "After Walter left for England that summer, I began dating your father . . . but then *he* went off to war, too." She sighed and her expression grew distant.

I didn't let her off the hook. "Did you give *Dad* the same 'nice' send-off?"

Mother's nose hiked up and her eyes

looked down. "I hardly see how that is any of your business. It's completely irrelevant to this discussion!"

It seemed to me that relations with the man who was my father (or at least who was supposed to be my father) were more my business than her mission of mercy with Walter Yeager. But Mother had her own rules regarding relevancy.

She gazed out the bedroom window, where Jack Frost had skated across the bottom of the pane, making an intricate icy pattern on the glass. "You know, I've never told another living soul about Walter and me," she murmured, serious and not at all arch. "Not even your father."

Mother closed her eyes, and I tucked the covers up around her, then tiptoed out.

Just another typical warm-and-fuzzy conversation between Mother and me, involving ancient sexual shenanigans and assorted secrets.

But I was worried about Mother . . . not her melancholy mood over Walter — that would pass. What really concerned me was her imagining that Walter had been murdered, and her desire to have it so. Despite the two incidents she and I had been involved in, murder was hardly the norm in a small town like Serenity.

Anyway, I had my hands full just keeping Mother busy with healthy concerns, and off the murder-go-round.

The next morning when I stuck my nose out the back door, it practically got frozen off — the weather had turned bitterly cold, the wind whipping drifts around so much that snow still seemed to be falling on what was otherwise a clear day. I put Shoosh down on the back stoop and told her it was okay to take care of business right there, which she understood, and proceeded to do-do in record time.

Mother was already up, and must have been for quite some time, because she had baked her famous Christmas Kringle coffee cake; its delicious aroma hung in the kitchen making my mouth water — and Sooshi's, too, the doggie doing a little begging dance at my feet. Since the Danish pastry didn't have a note stuck to it, saying to keep my mitts off, I felt free to cut myself a piece (and a tiny one for Soosh), then poured out a cup of hot java, and joined Mother at the dining room table, where she was looking at various copies of plays that were spread out before her.

Seasonal sidebar: We now interrupt this story to share with you Mother's Kringle recipe (but be forewarned — they apparently had a lot of time on their hands back in Denmark).

Danish Christmas Kringle

Batter:
3/4 cup butter
3 cups flour
3 Tbl. sugar
1 tsp. salt
1 package active dry yeast
3/4 cup milk
1 egg, beaten

Filling:
2 cups chopped pecans or walnuts
1 1/2 cup brown sugar
3/4 cup butter, softened

Glaze:
2 cups confectioner's sugar
2 Tbl. milk (more or less)
1 tsp. vanilla extract

In a large bowl, cut butter into the flour, sugar, and salt, to look like bread crumbs. Dissolve yeast in 1/4 cup warm water. Add the yeast, milk, and egg to the batter and beat until smooth. Chill two hours.

On a floured surface, roll dough to a twelve-inch square; fold and roll twice more.

Roll to 24 × 12-inch rectangle. Cut lengthwise in two strips (for two kringles) and spread each with filling. Roll to close and shape into ovals. Moisten edges and seal. Place seam sides down on greased baking sheets. Cover and let rise till twice its size, about 25 minutes.

Bake at 375 degrees for 25–30 minutes, or until golden brown. When cooled, drizzle glaze on top of the kringles.

I once tried to make that myself, but when I got to the "fold and roll twice more," I gave up and threw the dough outside for the animals. Then, to add insult to injury, not even the raccoons — who'll eat anything (don't ask) — would go near it.

And now back to our regularly scheduled chapter. . . .

Mother, in a much better mood, asked chirpily, "Which production do you think I should direct in February?"

The Playhouse was dark in January, as the local cast and crew took a much-needed break from the theater — and Mother.

I fingered through the pile, and selected one. "Why not Agatha Christie's *Murder Is Easy*?" I wasn't familiar with that particular play, but I'd never read or seen a Christie that hadn't been entertaining. And I figured if Mother got involved in a murder mystery in the theatrical world, she might not be so inclined to create one for herself out in the real one.

Mother's eyes danced. "Why not *indeed!* There's even a small part for me."

All the better to keep Mother busy, directing *and* acting.

Mother was saying, "I could play Lavinia Fullerton — even though she dies on page twenty. Of course I'd have to use heavy makeup to pass for such an elderly woman . . . but I *do* so love a death scene —"

Then Mother gasped, and I jumped in my chair, splattering coffee on the table. But she wasn't demonstrating a death scene, just making a discovery on the play's list-of-characters page.

"Why, there's also a nice part for *Chaz* as the local village girl who aids the amateur sleuth," Mother burbled. "She could give the play a nice ring of British authenticity."

I asked skeptically, "Are you sure Chaz is up to it? I mean, what experience has she had?"

Mother pawed the air with a scoffing hand. "Why are you always so negative? The girl's a *natural!* Besides, getting involved with the play will help take the poor dear girl's mind off her grandfather's murder."

I didn't bother to argue the murder point. And of course a comedy might be better suited for distracting Chaz from her gran'dad's death. But Mother's enthusiasm for Agatha Christie was unstoppable at this point.

Mother was on a roll. "Certainly some of the sets — like the train in the first act — will be challenging on our limited budget. . . . And wouldn't it be grand if a *real* automobile could seem to run my character over right there on stage? *That* would sure put the audience on their feet!"

Vivian Borne, hit by a car onstage? If word got out, the house would be packed every night. Give the people what they want, and they'll turn out. . . .

I drained what was left of my cup, and left Mother to her musings, thankful her attention was now on the new play.

After rinsing my dishes in the sink, I took my Prozac capsule from the plastic seven-day pill keeper I kept on the counter next to the coffeemaker. Mother had a pill caddy, too, and I checked to make sure she was current. She was, praise the Lord and pass the medication. Then I headed back upstairs to shower and get ready for my shopping date with Tina.

Teen and I met in high school, when I was a sophomore and she was a junior. I'd come around a hallway corner one day after school and found a bunch of senior girls bullying her. Not liking the odds, I jumped in with my fists clenched and my mouth flapping, and the bullies fled like cockroaches when somebody flips on the light switch. Tina and I have been best friends ever since.

Within an hour, my clothes were strewn all over the bedroom as if a tornado had hit. Everything I had put on was too tight, which meant that my fat bucket had overflowed.

Fat bucket, you ask? Glad to expound on the subject. . . .

Ever wonder why you can sometimes eat more than usual and not gain weight? Then one morning you wake up and BAM! there's an extra five pounds staring you in the face? That's because everybody has a fat bucket, and you're safe as long as it doesn't fill up and spill over (I usually hover perilously close to the rim). The reverse is also true; that's why it takes so long to lose weight, because that bucket of fat has to be depleted. So don't give up! Hang in there dieting a few more weeks, and one day you'll see results overnight. I hope this helps you.

I selected some black DKNY jeans that fit only because they contained two percent Lycra, a Gap gray hoodie with silver trim that scratched but had been on sale so I put up with it, and a pair of Kenzie black leather boots with cute side buttons that Tina passed along to me because they'd hurt her bunions. (They hurt *my* bunions, too, but one must at times suffer for the sake of fashion.) Then I traipsed downstairs.

Mother was gabbing on the phone, and by the gist of her end of the conversation, seemed to be already putting the play into motion. I blew her a kiss, then threw on my black wool peacoat, and headed out to my cold car.

Tina and her husband, Kevin, lived in a white ranch-style home on a bluff overlooking the Mississippi River, a great view, especially in winter when the trees were bare. In another month, when the eagles swooped down from the frozen North to the not-so-frozen Midwest to hunt for fish in the churning river, Tina and Kevin would get out their binoculars and become avid eagle-watchers. (I like to watch, too — for maybe five minutes.)

Usually, Tina picked me up for our shopping sprees, but since we were hitting the stores at Indian Mounds Mall, which was closer to her than me, I was the designated driver.

I pulled into the mouth of their driveway, where Kevin's sporty silver Mazda was parked next to Tina's black Lexus, which meant that Kev — a pharmaceutical salesman — was home for the day. Kev, a sandy-haired hunk of thirty-three, was a great guy, and always nice to me, even when I got my BFF into a bit of trouble now and then.

Tina and Kevin had been trying to have children for the last few years, and then a month ago Tina discovered she had uterine cancer (thankfully caught early), which derailed their plans for a family. She and I had talked about this only once, over wine, late into a night, when she'd revealed that she and Kev were exploring adoption or possibly trying to find a surrogate mother, although Teen was on the fence about either option, afraid her cancer might recur.

So, naturally, I was anxious to see how my BFF was doing, even though our conversation today would be limited to conspicuous consuming.

I was about to honk, when Tina came out, slamming the front door behind her. She looked great, as usual, the winter sun highlighting her natural, golden-blond hair, making a halo effect around her Nordic features. She was wearing the same black jeans as me (but a size smaller), her white Michael Kors leather jacket (she saw it first), and a girlie-pink Betsey Johnson wool scarf (I had one in blue).

Tina hopped in the passenger side, said, "Let's do this," and I put the pedal to the metal.

Indian Mounds was an outdoor mall just a short five minutes away, but across the treacherous bypass. A stoplight, however, had been recently installed at our juncture after a state senator's wife got in a car crash while trying to cross the busy, four-lane highway on her way to a white sale. (Wife, minor bruising; Cadillac Escalade, totaled.) And I mean to say, that traffic light went in practically overnight.

On the way, Tina and I negotiated having lunch first — no sense shopping on an empty stomach — and we arrived at Michael's, an upscale Italian eatery, just before noon. Even though the place was hopping with business types and holiday shoppers, we managed to snag one of the last cherry-wood booths. After we both ordered a small Caesar salad, minestrone soup, and a glass of white wine, Tina and I settled in for our preshopping gabfest, as only amateurs talk while they shop.

I said, "First, tell me how you're doing. . . ."

Tina's smile looked a little forced. "Oh, fine . . . just fine. I'm seeing another specialist after Christmas. I want to know all of my options." Her smile turned sad. "Of course the one option I *really* want — to have a baby of my own — I can't have."

Somewhere in the restaurant an infant was crying, underscoring Tina's words.

I reached across the table and clasped her hand. "I'm so sorry, honey. I wish there was something I could do. . . ."

What I had said was heartfelt, even if it did sound a little lame, at least to me.

Tina forced another smile. "But we can still adopt. Outside the country if need be."

I nodded. "And it'll be just like your own."

It? Just like your own? Lame, again. That kid was still crying, the little ham.

My thoughts turned to Jake, and what it felt like to look at his face and see part of me, and Roger, and how in some way I'd taken my son's existence for granted. And here was my best friend, unable to have a child, and wanting one so badly.

Tina was saying, "Enough of me. Brandy, I want to know how *you* are doing."

The ball being tossed into my court I took to mean Teen didn't care to talk any further about her cancer treatment, or adoption.

I said only, "Just peachy keen — what could ever be sunnier than life with Vivian Borne?"

She smiled, catching my drift — I didn't want to talk about my problems, either.

Sometimes, the best things friends can do for each other is keep the conversation light and cheerful, rather than throw a "pity party."

The wine arrived, and after a few sips, Tina and I got down to really important subjects.

"What's your opinion of regifting?" Tina asked.

I set down my glass of wine. "I used to think it was tacky . . . but now, because of conservation and recycling, who's to say you're not doing something positive?"

"Oooo. I like this. Regifting is *green!*"

I raised a cautionary finger. "That is, it's acceptable *if* a certain protocol is followed."

"Such as?"

"Well, it goes without saying that the gift you want to recycle should fit the person you're passing it on to. You know, don't give a country-western CD to someone who likes hip-hop."

"Naturally," Tina said with a crisp nod.

"And the item should be rewrapped in a

plain box — so the getter doesn't know what store it came from and can't take it back. Also, be sure to check for any telltale sign that the gift was originally yours . . . like an enclosure card addressed to you."

"Ouch. Anything else?"

Another cautionary finger wag. "Always regift *outside* your own circle of family and friends . . . otherwise, you could receive it back the next year."

Tina smiled. "That *has* happened to us. Kevin's brother once gave us this horrible hot dog cooker —"

I laughed, "No! Not that as-seen-on-TV contraption that electrocutes wieners?"

"That's the one. And the first — and *only* — time we used it . . . honestly, Brandy, our lights dimmed!"

She waited for my giggle fit to subside.

"Well," Teen went on, "we passed it on to one of Kevin's sisters, who has a bunch of kids — kids love hot dogs, right? And she sent us a thank-you note saying how much they all adored it. Then the following Christmas, bang, we get it back!"

"Where's it now?"

"Kev was afraid I'd try to get rid of it again, at a garage sale or something. He disappeared with it. Probably buried the thing in the backyard."

Our food arrived and we crunched our salads and slurped our soups.

After splitting the bill, Tina went off to use the bathroom, and I made my way back through the boisterous crowd to the front entrance to wait for her.

I passed the time noting what the women coming in and out of the restaurant were wearing — holiday sweaters ran two to one — when someone gave my arm a little tug.

I turned to find Mrs. Lange, Joe's mother, a short, plump, nervous lady who reminded me of Aunt Bea on the old Andy Griffin TV show, only not so cheerful. She had on the official red and purple colors of the Red-Hat Social Club, whose only mandate was to eat and have fun. By the bread crumbs on the woman's sweater, she indeed was eating . . . but by her frown-creased forehead, she wasn't having much fun.

"Brandy, dear, have you seen Joe lately?" Mrs. Lange asked anxiously.

I nodded. "Just yesterday, at the clinic."

"How did he seem to you . . . I mean, mentally?" Her right eye had developed a tic, making her question unintentionally comic.

"Why, fine, I guess. We had a nice conversation. Why do you ask? Isn't he living at home with you, Mrs. Lange?"

She took a deep breath that quivered when it came back out. "When I got up this morning, he was gone — along with his army fatigues and all of his gear."

That didn't sound good. I'd never known Joe to suit up during the winter.

Mrs. Lange asked, "You're *sure* he seemed all right?"

I frowned in thought. "Pleasant . . . talkative . . . yeah, fine. We spoke about going to the flea market for a while. Then I had to go in for my appointment." I paused, then asked, "Have you spoken to his therapist?"

The woman nodded, the brim of her red hat flapping as if in agreement. "The doctor also said my son was in good spirits, so I don't understand *what* could have set him off."

I had no answer, either. "I'll certainly call you if I see him around, or hear of anything."

The woman forced a smile. "Thank you, Brandy."

As I watched Mrs. Lange return to the table of chattering red-hatted ladies, I spotted Tina talking to a middle-aged, businessman-type who was having a martini lunch at the bar. Teen caught my eye and gave me a "Sorry" look, meaning she had gotten stalled coming out of the ladies' room and had to stop-and-chat, a consequence of her Tourism Office position.

I nodded back as if I understood when, truth be told, no man, woman, or business should ever stand in the way of sales at the mall. That was when I noticed Peggy Sue — dressed head to toe in expensive Burberry — seated alone in a nearby booth.

Since the table was set for two, Sis was probably waiting for someone — which couldn't be Uncle Bob, because he always worked through the lunch hour (to pay for items like that Burberry ensemble!), so it had to be one of those venomous gal-pals of hers, so notorious for keeping Peggy Sue waiting.

On impulse (as if I ever acted any other way), I headed over. Maybe this was the opportunity I'd been looking for, if not to broach the subject of my real parentage, at least to set a time when she and I could get together to discuss it calmly.

And so, feeling full of good pre-Christmas cheer, I stopped at the booth and chirped, "Hi, Peggy Sue!"

Sis looked up, startled, as if the ghost of Christmas Past had suddenly materialized. "Brandy . . . what are you doing here?"

Yes, the warmth my sister exuded toward

me was like the traditional Christmas hearth embodied in one wonderful human being.

"It's the mall," I said, as if that explained everything, which it should have. "Just had lunch with Tina. And now we're going shopping." I slid into the empty side of the booth. "Peggy Sue . . . there's something I've been wanting to talk to you about. . . ."

Sis seemed anxious; her eyes were wandering, looking past me, toward the entrance of the restaurant. "Well, what is it?" she asked with a smile so brittle it barely qualified as one.

Suddenly, my nerve, along with my good cheer, evaporated. "Well, if you're *too busy*. . . ."

"I *am* meeting someone," Sis said stiffly. "Can't it wait?"

"Sure," I mumbled, "it can wait. It's already waited thirty-one years. . . ."

Sis was frowning at me, confused, not angry, when a dark figure loomed over us: the ghost of Christmas Future, aka Connie Grimes, cocooned in a long, black puffy-coat, which only emphasized her considerable girth.

So the over-Botoxed bovine was Peggy Sue's luncheon date, and the reason for Sis's anxiety at my showing up out of the blue. She feared another altercation between

Connie and me — after all, I was one shoving match shy of a restraining order.

But before I could stick the first needle in, Connie asked me, "Did I just see you talking to that . . ." She made a face. ". . . Mrs. Lange?"

I was still seated in the booth, and Peggy Sue nudged me with her knee to vacate.

"Yeah," I said, sliding out. "What about her?"

Connie had taken off her coat, and tossed it in ahead of her as she assumed my spot. "Not *her* . . . she can't help having a crazy *son* like that, I suppose. Isn't he a . . . friend of yours?"

"Yes . . ." I didn't know where this was going. Maybe I was overwhelmed by so much charm.

Connie said smugly, "I hear he's gone loony tunes again. Which explains why he nearly *killed* me the other day."

Not that anyone needed a reason to kill Connie Grimes. I nonetheless was interested in hearing what the woman had to say.

So I asked, "What do you mean, Connie?"

She looked from me to an uncomfortable Peggy Sue, then back again. "Well," she said huffily, "I was driving in to that awful trailer park in South End last night, with the DAR girls . . ." Connie paused to explain to dumb little me. ". . . Daughters of the Revolution?"

"Yes," I said primly.

"Well, we were taking Christmas turkeys to some of the underprivileged people who live there — we do that *every* year, that's just the way the Serenity Daughters are — and that *maniac* Joe Lange came driving out like a *maniac,* and nearly hit us."

That was two maniacs, but I didn't say anything. I was busy having a cold feeling fill the pit of my stomach.

So there I stood with the woman I was convinced was sending me poison-pen notes, and the other woman who I was even more convinced was my biological mother, and here's what I did about it.

"You girls enjoy your lunch," I said, and caught up at the bar with Tina, who'd finished her conversation with the business acquaintance.

"Saw you talking with your sister and Connie Grimes," she said, looping her arm in mine as we headed toward the exit onto the mall.

"Lucky me."

As we passed Mrs. Lange, seated with a tableful of chattering red-hatted ladies, Tina whispered, "Something wrong with your friend Joe? Saw you and Mrs. Lange talking."

"Joe seems to have fallen off the mental-health wagon, for no good reason."

"Could be the holidays," she offered.

"Maybe," I said.

Who *didn't* this time of year drive insane?

Banishing from my mind any suspicions of Joe and that Tarzan book of Mr. Yeager's he coveted, I followed Tina out of the restaurant and we headed straight for Ingram's, our favorite store. With Christmas and Hanukkah mere weeks away, the discounts were already deep, and Tina and I cruised silently through each department, picking up bargains, crossing names off our lists.

About an hour later, we were down to *us*, and took a second pass around the store with an eye on what we might get each other. This round, we allowed talking, but only a few words, like when I picked up a cute pointy-toed stiletto I thought Tina might like, and she went, "Ow!" And then she pointed out a sparkly silver V-neck sweater, and after copping a feel, I went, "Itchy-scratchy." But soon Tina and I got enough "Ooohs" and "Aaahs" from each other that we had some real gift possibilities. Then Tina said she wanted to go to the lingerie department for a bra, and I suggested that while she did that, I'd visit the stationery section for Christmas cards. A total ploy on both our parts, of course, Tina doubling back to the junior department to buy me the Rock N Republic jeans I'd squealed at, while I sneaked over to the shoes section to get her the UGG boots she'd drooled over. Why do we even bother with the subterfuge?

Because it's fun, maybe?

We had arranged to meet at the front entrance, but I took a detour by the cosmetics counter to replace my dried-up mascara.

Just before Christmas is the best time to visit the cosmetics counter to try out new products and get personalized attention — not to mention free samples — because everybody else is frantically running around buying presents in the other departments. (The exception is the perfume counter, where herds of husbands and boyfriends roam the aisle like confused cattle, trying to decipher one scent from the other.)

Here are three makeup tips for women no longer in their twenties:

1) Less is more. . . *way* less — like the very first time you wore cosmetics and tried to fool your folks. The

more greasepaint you pile on, the older and harder you look.

2) Buy expensive cosmetics, not because they are exceptionally better than the drugstore variety, but because you will feel prettier when you apply your Chanel Rouge Allure in "Romantic." That sounds like an opinion, but I swear it's a fact.

3) Work on improving your personality; as beauty fades, a woman can't get away with as much nonsense.

I had just purchased the mascara (brown — a tip from Bette Davis) when I spotted my old pal Pudgy — the book scout from the flea market encounter — in the adjacent fine jewelry department, where an attractive, young black woman in a clingy gray dress was in the process of showing him a watch at the David Yurman counter.

I sauntered over and pretended to look at the other pricey pieces in the glass display case next to him.

Pudgy, wearing the same silly plaid topcoat as the other night, was saying, "What about *that* one. . . ." He tapped the glass with a fat finger.

The saleswoman opened the back of the

glass case and withdrew another watch, which she placed on a square piece of white velvet to show off the diamonds better — as if.

"You certainly have a tasteful eye, sir." She smiled.

Which didn't explain his coat.

"How much?" the book scout asked.

"Forty-nine hundred."

Pudgy didn't blink; but I sure did. That was a lot of cabbage to wrap around your wrist.

Without a pause, the man said, "I'll take it."

Now the saleslady blinked — not at the high-end purchase, but the wad of hundred-dollar bills Pudgy was producing from his wallet.

"It *is* a beautiful watch," she said, recovering, "Mister, uh . . . ?"

"Potthoff, Harry Potthoff."

Not exactly Bond, James Bond.

"Well, Mr. Potthoff," the saleswoman cooed, "you're *certainly* going to make some woman very happy."

"I assume you will wrap it at no extra charge." It was a statement, not a question.

Now, I happen to know that wrapping *wasn't* free at Ingram's — even for a five-grand watch — and you could expect to stand in a long line back in customer service.

But the saleslady, sensing a deal-breaker (and the loss of a hefty commission), only said sweetly, "Why, of course, Mr. Potthoff!" She called another clerk over to take her place at the counter, then ran off to handle the wrapping, personally.

Tina, looking as hot-in-her-coat and tired as I felt, and laden with heavy shopping bags, trundled toward me. "I've been looking all over for you! We were supposed to meet at the front door!"

"Well, you were late so I came over here," I whined.

"*I* was right on time," she snapped. "*You* were early. . . ."

(FYI: Tina and I are often crabby by the end of our shopping sprees.)

The cold outside air, however, cooled our tempers, and by the time we loaded up my car, all was forgiven.

Even though it was only five o'clock, the sky was dark when I dropped Tina off at her house. I let the car idle in the driveway while we sorted the various packages in the backseat, making sure we each had our own booty.

Then Tina said sweetly, "Thanks, Brandy, I had a really nice time."

"Me, too," I smiled. "Let's do it again . . . for the *after*-Christmas sales."

I waited in the car while Tina made it to her front door, where Kevin — after giving me a wave — helped her in with the packages.

I sat for another minute in the drive. I could see them through the front window as they stood in the living room, Tina with her arms around Kevin, head on his shoulder, and he stroking her hair.

Then an impulse hit me, and I would be darned if I'd let this opportunity pass me by like the one with Peggy Sue had. I shut off the engine, hopped out of the car, hurried up the sidewalk, banged on the door.

Tina answered. She was smiling, but her eyes were red. "Did you forget something?" she asked. "Or did I?"

I stepped inside. "No, I forgot something. . . . Something important I want to tell you and Kevin."

Hearing this, Kevin joined us in the foyer. He put an arm around his wife's shoulders and said, "Hiya, Brandy. What is it?"

Tina, with a combination of puzzlement and concern asked, "What *is* it, honey?"

"I just wanted to tell you guys," I said, "that if you need a surrogate mom? I'd be glad to have your baby for you."

A TRASH 'N' TREASURES TIP

A flea market is the easiest place to begin a collection because quantity is high and prices are low. In deciding *what* to collect, consider price range, difficulty in acquiring more pieces, and — most important of all — space constraints. Mother once started collecting old wringer washing machines until she ran out of room in a week.

CHAPTER FOUR:
SEARCH AND SEIZURE

After leaving a stunned Tina and Kevin standing in their foyer after my surprise offer, I returned home, where (in the privacy of my bedroom) I celled the one person in the world whose permission I wanted before proceeding any further.

My ex-husband, Roger, answered.

"Brandy . . . anything wrong?"

"Does there have to be something wrong for me to call?"

"Of course not. . . ."

"Good. 'Cause I'm fine. Thanks for asking. Is Jake around?"

"He's in his room on his PS-3."

"Early Christmas present?" I asked. During Jake's stay with me in October, the upcoming release of the expensive video game system was all the boy could talk about.

"Yeah, afraid I couldn't wait."

"You mean *Jake* couldn't wait, and was

making your life miserable."

He chuckled softly. "You got that right."

"How long did you have to stand in line?"

Roger sighed. "Don't even *go* there. . . . Let's just say midnight at a Wal-Mart is proof of life after death, because there must be a heaven since for sure hell exists."

I laughed, then said, "I know Jake hates being interrupted in the middle of a game, but would you get him, please? Kind of important."

"Sure," he said. "Expect to wait a while, though. . . ."

I knew Roger was right, and had come prepared; I used the time to untangle a bunch of chain necklaces from my jewelry box.

Then my son's voice was in my ear. "Hey, Mom, what's up?"

"Sorry to bother, honey, but I have something to ask you that I just didn't think was right for an e-mail."

"Oh-kay. . . ."

"You know my best friend Tina?"

"Ah-huh."

I explained, as best as I could, that because of her cancer, Tina and her husband wouldn't be able to have children of their own.

With all the compassion a kid his age

could summon, which wasn't very much, Jake said, "Gee, that's too bad." Then: "Is that all you wanted to tell me? You upset about that and, uh, need to talk or something?" He wanted to get back to his game.

"No, there's more. . . . They *can* have a baby with my help. But not if *you* don't want me to." I paused, then asked, "Do you know what a surrogate mother is?"

"Hummm . . ." In my mind's eye I could see Jake wrinkling his cute, freckled nose in thought. "I think so," he said slowly. "Saw something on the Discovery Channel. Kinda like a lady bakes a cake in her oven from somebody else's batter, right?"

I laughed. "That's pretty darn close. And I want to do that for them."

There was silence, then Jake asked, "Does this mean I'll have a little brother or sister?"

This was what I was afraid of. "No, even though I'm the mom, you won't be related. After the baby's born, it will belong to Tina and her husband."

"So I don't have to share a room or, you know, my stuff or anything with this newbie?"

"No."

"Good!"

I had counted on Jake's self-interest to win his approval. "Then you don't have any objection?"

"Naw. Sounds like a really nice thing for you to do. . . . Knock yourself out, Mom."

Downstairs, I found Mother seated at the dining room table, furiously making notes on a yellow legal pad.

She looked up, her magnified eyes behind the glasses dancing a wild jig, her hair frozen in its own bizarre dance step. "I know who would be *perfect* to cast as the male lead in the Christie play . . . but he can be *awfully* temperamental, and somewhat undependable."

"Glad it's coming together."

Mother studied me. "Something wrong, dear? You're frowning. You're making wrinkles!"

I plastered on a smile guaranteed to make even more lines. "No! Everything's fine."

(You didn't think for a moment that I would tell *Mother* about my surrogacy offer, did you? If so, you're either a new reader or not paying attention. Good Lord, it would be all over town before Tina and Kevin even had a chance to think it over.)

I said, "I take it you want to go out for dinner."

Mother smiled up at me. "How did you know, dear?"

"Because it's almost six and there's no

yummy smells coming from the kitchen."

All right, I'll admit that my using words like "yummy" had something to do with my mother treating me like a child.

"You see, dear! As much as you try to resist it, your natural sleuthing skills are a part of you." Mother brushed the legal pad aside. "How about going to that new Mexican restaurant you've been wanting to try?"

This surprised me, as Mother doesn't care for spicy food because the resulting indigestion almost inevitably keeps her up all night watching Home Shopping Network. And I don't care for the bills we get for the vitamin complexes, exercise gizmos, and kitchen miracles that ensue, so I hadn't pressed my Mexican yen.

Nonetheless, I said, "Great! But I'll have to give Sushi *her* food, first." I glanced around for the dog, who should have come trotting in at the sound of the word "food."

"I've already taken care of the little darling," Mother informed me.

"You have?"

She lifted her chin, eyes sparkling with pride. "*And* given her her shot of insulin."

"You *did?*"

Mother had only done that once before, when I was too sick to get out of bed with a migraine; she has an abject fear of needles (slightly less so when it's someone else getting stuck).

I narrowed my eyes. "All right . . . what's going on? My natural sleuthing skills tell me you're up to something."

Both her hands came up in "Lawsy, Miss Scarlet" fashion. "Why, nothing, dear! It's simply that you've seemed so *very* down in the dumps lately, and I only wanted to please." She gave me the kind of smile a bank teller gives a holdup man. "The idea that my gesture might be anything other than heartfelt . . . well, it wounds me, dear . . . right here." She thumped her chest.

As if anything could pierce that egotistical heart.

But to keep the peace, I said, "Forgive me, Mother," and trundled off to get our raccoon coats. It only seemed fair to warn the world we were coming.

On the drive to the Mexican restaurant, Mother chattered on and on about her plans for the new production, and — as with most of her one-sided conversations — I had to either rise to her level of enthusiasm, or fade back entirely. Not having the energy, I chose the latter.

Mother, tiring of own voice for a change, began to sing "Aba Daba Honeymoon," which if you've never heard it (or even if

107

you have) is about a monkey and a chimp and consists mostly of the words "aba" and "daba." Which pretty much summed up our relationship these days.

La Hacienda was located in South End, and everything on the menu sounded both authentic and delicious. Not knowing when I'd have an opportunity to be back, I ordered guacamole (made directly at our table), chiles rellenos, Spanish rice, refried beans, and for dessert, flan. Fat bucket be damned.

Mother questioned the poor waitress exhaustively about all of the dishes, and what was in them, asking her in her best John McLaughlin fashion to assign a relative hotness on a scale of one to ten (ten being "metaphysical hotness"), finally making me kick her under the table to let up.

After glaring at me, Mother ordered huevos rancheros, but when they arrived (the orders came quickly), she merely picked at her food, pushing the spicy eggs around her plate as if rearranging furniture. Apparently, she wasn't in the mood for a night of Home Shopping Network.

Which was fine with me, because I would never be in the mood for the credit-card bill that would follow.

As I was taking my last bite of the delicious syrup-topped custard, the bedraggled waitress came over to ask if we wanted anything else, and Mother said, "*Sí!* An order of beef tacos to go."

As the waitress trotted off, I asked, puzzled, "A midnight snack to watch while Suzanne Somers sells you an exercise device, or Ernest Borgnine's wife peddles you some perfume?"

She gave me a primly offended look. "The tacos are not for *us,* dear."

I put down my fork, the custard curdling on my palate. "Well, they're certainly not for Sushi."

Mother neatly folded her paper napkin as if it were quality linen, placed it on the table, and said matter-of-factly, "I thought, as long as we're down here, in this part of town, we could just stop by and see how your little friend Chaz is getting along."

At last, the real motive for dining at La Hacienda reared its bug-eyed head. The order-to-go reflected a standard Mother strategy: She rarely dropped in on anyone uninvited without bringing something along to take the sting out of her sudden appearance . . . even if said item was unwarranted, unneeded, and unwanted.

I asked fractiously, "What if Chaz doesn't like tacos? Or would rather have chicken than beef? Did you ever think maybe she's a vegetarian?"

Mother's expression turned sour. "Brandy, sometimes I wonder why I bother doing *anything* nice for you!"

I raised twin palms in surrender. "Okay, I appreciate it, you letting me try out La Hacienda. I've been wanting to."

She nodded smugly.

"But, Mother, there was no cause for turning it into the D-Day Landing. I'd like to know how Chaz is doing myself. I don't need to be tricked or handled."

Mother blinked. "Oh. All right, dear, I will try to remember that. From now on, I will endeavor to be as straightforward as possible. I will indulge in neither subterfuge nor sophistry. I will . . . what were talking about?"

"Beats me."

The tacos came, we paid the check, and left.

A few minutes later, I turned at the convenience store into Happy Trails Trailer Court, driving down the icy, main lane, the Christmas lights and yard decorations lending red and green twinkles to a landscape otherwise dominated by sludgy snow. Up ahead, I spotted a police car parked in front of Mr. Yeager's mobile home, and I put on the brakes, skidding a little.

Mother and I exchanged alarmed looks.

"Yikes," we both said.

I drove on slowly, easing my Buick in behind the squad car. We got out, and I climbed the couple of steps to the door, Mother waiting below, holding the sack of food. I knocked.

Chaz opened the door immediately, which startled both Mother and me — it was as if the girl had been standing there, waiting for us. She stepped aside for us to get in out of the cold.

"Is anything wrong?" I asked the girl.

"Your *mate's* 'ere," Chaz said, nodding toward a familiar figure.

Brian, standing stiffly in the little living room, seemed none too happy to see us, and I didn't think Mother's steaming sack of tacos was going to turn the tide.

"What's going on?" Mother demanded, as if she were in charge. Tact, it should be noted, was in my mother's opinion something that one put on the teacher's chair.

Brian took a few steps toward her. "Frankly, Mrs. Borne," he said, his boyish handsome face as tight as his terse words, "this is police business, and not any of yours."

If I had a dollar for every time something

of that sort had been said to Mother by the Serenity PD in the last year, we could have afforded tacos for the entire force.

Chaz offered cheerfully, " 'E came to tell me the chief inspector 'imself wants to talk to me *downtown,* 'cause I'm an interesting person, innit?"

"You mean a 'person of interest,' dear," Mother corrected.

Chaz screwed up her face. "Eh? That's wha' I said!"

I said, "Chaz, a 'person of interest' is just a politically correct way of calling somebody a suspect." I looked at Brian. "A suspect in what? If this is about that *bank* bag —"

"It's not," Brian said testily. He narrowed his eyes and lowered his head, letting me know somehow that he wasn't just irritated as an officer, but just plain irritated. "That doesn't mean I won't want to talk to you later, Brandy, about how conveniently that missing money showed up."

I muttered, "Okay . . . ah, sure," and faded behind Mother, who had pulled herself up to her full five feet eight inches (she used to be five-nine, but has shrunk a little — I knew the feeling, since I'd shrunk to about three foot two ever since Brian gave me that irritated look).

"This girl has rights, you know," Mother

snapped, "even if she *is* a second-class citizen in this country!"

"Yeah!" an emboldened Chaz retorted. "I'm second-class, innit? Best you *'member* that, mate."

Mother continued haughtily, "And I'm sure the *British embassy* would be none too pleased to hear of any police brutality that was waged against one of Her Majesty's loyal subjects."

Chaz said, "Yeah!" Then, "Wha'? No! *Don't* call 'em! I jumped me parole when I came 'ere —"

Brian's eyes had a sort of deadness as he fixed them on Mother. "It may come as a surprise to you, Mrs. Borne, that we don't have a British embassy in Serenity."

I said, "But Chaz *does* have certain rights —"

"Settle down, all of you!" Brian put both hands up like a traffic cop. Then he turned to Chaz. "No one is accusing you of anything. We just want to ask you a few routine questions down at the station . . . to clarify and expand on earlier statements you made, so that we can close the file on your grandfather."

This was pure B.S., but I had to admit Brian had delivered it convincingly.

Chaz looked from Brian to me to Mother,

and back again.

"All right," she said, "but if I don't like the sound of the questions, I'm gonna get me a solicitor, yeah?"

Brian nodded. "Fair enough. And the sooner we go to the station, the sooner you'll be back home."

Mother said, "Don't say anything without a lawyer, dear! This is a murder investigation!"

"No," Brian said, "it is not. We're investigating a suspicious death, and —"

"There!" Mother said, raising a triumphant finger like an old-time politician making a point. "*Suspicious!* He's said it himself!"

Chaz turned to me. "Bran, what should I do?"

"Go with Officer Lawson. You can trust him. She can trust you, can't she, Brian?"

"Certainly . . . Brandy, a word?"

Brian took me deeper into the living room. "I want you to promise me that you and your mother aren't getting involved in this thing."

"Why?" I said. Not being a smart aleck, just wanting to know. "*Is* it a 'thing'? Is Mother right?"

"Your Mother is seldom right, but even if she were, you and she are going to get

114

yourselves in real trouble if this doesn't stop. This Nancy Drew meets Jessica Fletcher crap has to cease, understood?"

"That's not very nice."

"No. It isn't. And now you're going. Both of you."

Then for the second time, Mother and I were unceremoniously tossed out of the trailer.

But before we left, Mother held out the sack of tacos and told Chaz, up in the doorway, what she'd brought.

"Tacos! Brilliant! Thanks, luv! Okay if I nosh on these on the way downtown, Officer?"

"Sure," Brian said.

Chaz came down and got the sack and Brian followed, closing the door behind them.

From our car, we watched Brian put Chaz in the back of the police car, and, to make sure we did leave, he signaled for me to drive off first, and followed behind us.

As we exited the mouth of the trailer court, a black sedan was pulling in. Mother glanced over her shoulder as the vehicle passed, twisting her neck so much that it cracked as if a chiropractor had been involved.

"Did you see who that *was?*" she exclaimed.

"No." I had my eyes on the icy road.

"Quick!" she said. "Pull into that convenience store . . . I need milk."

I was exhausted, and exasperated. "But we've *got* milk, Mother . . . I bought some the other day."

"Then . . . I need butter."

We had that, too, but I could see where this was going, and mine was not to reason why, mine was but to do or strangle my mother; so I did as I was told. While I let the car idle, Mother got out and scampered into the store. That's right, scampered.

After a minute she returned with . . . nothing.

"What? No butter?" I asked. I wasn't surprised, of course, but I couldn't give her a completely free pass.

She gave me a long-suffering look. "Honestly, Brandy, sometimes you can be ever so slow on the uptake. Now that we've shaken Officer Lawson, I want you to turn around and go back."

"What *for?*" I asked.

Mother gave me a stare hard enough to crack a mirror.

I gave her one back. "Brian says we're going to get in trouble if we get involved in this."

"Do you think Mr. Yeager was murdered, dear?"

"Not really, no." I hadn't shared with her my fears that Joe Lange might have been involved, somehow, with the old gent's passing. My Prozac hadn't allowed me to even mull it over much myself.

"Well, then, since it's not a murder, what harm does it do, humoring your eccentric old mother?"

Referring to herself as "eccentric" and "old" was not an admission — that was Vivian Borne–style sarcasm.

So, as you damn well know I did, I drove the car back down the main road of the trailer court, and as we got closer to Mr. Yeager's mobile home, Mother bounced up and down in her seat like a child on a long trip spotting the first service station bathroom in miles.

"I *thought* that's who it was," she said excitedly.

In the short driveway of Yeager's trailer, two men in black topcoats were retrieving equipment from the open trunk of their sedan.

My eyes were wide, and my mouth yawned, but not because I was tired. "As Chaz might say, crikey. Those are crime scene guys."

117

"That's right." Mother's eyes shown as brightly as my car headlights. "Now slow down as we pass," she instructed.

I was already going at a snail's pace, and as we crawled by, Mother powered down her window and shouted ever so pleasantly, "I hope you boys have a *war*-rant!"

I cringed behind the wheel, then snarled, "*Mother!* Do you have to make trouble?"

And I hit the gas.

Mother sat back, huffing, "Well, they *better* have. But I bet they didn't even bother! Brandy, they were tricking that poor girl. Your *boyfriend* was tricking her!"

"Do you have to rub it in?"

Rather than drive by again, I searched for a back way out of the court.

Mother was sneering, " 'To clarify earlier statements' my foot! Your precious Brian wanted that girl out of the way so those test-tube gestapo agents could search that trailer. This *proves* Mr. Yeager was murdered!"

"Okay, looks like you may be right," I admitted. I had found the back exit of the trailer court. "What got you suspicious?"

Mother smiled grandly. "Because *I* attempted to give the poor man artificial respiration, and in doing so smelled the distinct odor of bitter almonds — the signature of cyanide!"

"You know this how? Did I miss the part where you went to pharmacy college?"

"Agatha *Christie* was a pharmacist's nurse, and I've read every one of her mysteries, at least twice!"

"And you didn't tell anyone about this?"

She harrumphed. "What *good* would it do? No one would listen. Everyone but you seems to think I'm just a crazy old woman!"

She had a point, except for the part about excluding me.

I frowned. "Where does someone even *get* cyanide, nowadays? On the Internet?"

Raising an eyebrow, Mother said, "Not without a great deal of red tape. After all, I should *know* — I've already tried."

"Tell me you didn't!"

"But I just said that I did."

"When?"

"The other day." Mother sighed, shrugged; how hard it was for her, bearing the weight of the world on her shoulders. "But there was a thirty-day wait for the cyanide, and endless questions. Then, when the computer asked me what I was going to use it for, and I typed in 'murder,' they *disconnected* me! How insufferably rude!"

I groaned. "Please tell me you didn't do this on *my* computer. . . ."

"Well, of *course,* dear. *I* certainly don't have one."

One more entry in the FBI file of Brandy Borne, compliments of Mother — if we were lucky. We might get a knock on the door from who-knows-who in law enforcement.

Mother was musing, "Of course, I probably *could* get my hands on cyanide if I wanted to."

"Please . . . you're starting to scare me."

She went on almost dreamily, "I dare say there's still some up in the rafters of our garage outside . . ."

"Huh?"

". . . among your father's old photography equipment. I've saved everything for years . . . even the old chemicals. You know how sentimental I am, dear."

I frowned at her. "You mean cyanide is used in photography?"

Mother shook her head. "Not these days. Deemed too dangerous. You know, your father nearly died once when he got it on his hands."

"When was this?"

"Oh, a long time ago, dear . . . when he used to develop his own pictures."

We were finally home, after a long, trying day . . .

. . . that wasn't over yet.

I should have known that something was wrong when Sushi didn't greet us at the door as we came in, stomping the snow from our boots, signaling our arrival to the sharp-eared pooch. I called her name, then went into the kitchen, expecting to find the dog sound asleep in her fluffy little bed.

And Sushi was there, all right, in her bed, but motionless, her pink tongue lolled out. I ran to her, dropped to my knees, and picked up the limp dog.

"Mother!" I screamed. "Something's wrong with Sushi!"

Mother rushed in, and bent over us.

"Oh, my," Mother said, fingers to her cheek, eyes huge behind the lenses. "She doesn't look at *all* well. I wonder if . . . ?"

"*What* do you wonder?"

"I wonder if I gave her the correct amount of insulin."

"How much did you give her?"

"Now, let me think. . . ." Mother put a fingertip to her lips.

"How *much,* Mother?"

She nodded crisply. "Sixteen units. Just like the instructions on the bottle said."

"That's *six* units, Mother! Only *six!*"

"Oh, dear me . . . I'm at fault, then. I simply must get these glasses checked."

I was sobbing. "She's overdosed." Cradling Sushi, I rocked her back and forth. "She's dead . . . she's dead, Mother, and you *killed* her!"

A TRASH 'N' TREASURES TIP

Before heading out to a flea market, prepare a list of items you're looking for, with notations on how much you're willing to pay. Share this list with friends . . . only make sure they understand the "willing to pay" part. One eager pal went ahead and bought me the Bakelite bracelet I desired, and I *still* owe her two payments.

Chapter Five: Arrested Development

As I sat on the kitchen floor with a limp Sushi in my arms, Mother said, "We must act quickly! I know a home remedy we can try that might bring her around. Once, an aunt of mine gave herself too much insulin and —"

"*Antidote,* Mother, not *anecdote!* For God's sake, just do it!"

I watched through tearful eyes as Mother rummaged in the cupboards, tossing food items left and right; then, finding what she was looking for, she dropped down on the floor beside me.

"Open her mouth, dear," Mother commanded, uncapping a bottle of Kayo Syrup.

I gently pried Sushi's lifeless jaws apart.

Pouring the sweet syrup on her fingers, Mother proceeded to rub the sticky goo on Sushi's gums, upper mouth, and tongue.

We waited.

Nothing.

Mother tried again.

"Oh, please, *please* . . ." I prayed, searching for any sign of life.

Suddenly, Sushi's little tongue flicked.

I let out a whoop!

"We're not out of the woods yet," Mother warned, raising a wiggling forefinger. "But this *will* help until we can transport the little darling to the vet. I'll go phone ahead now. . . ."

As the minutes passed, Sushi began to come slowly around, as her body absorbed the syrup, which in turn raised her blood sugar.

I could hear Mother on the phone in the living room, and after several endless moments, she returned. "Dr. Tillie said to bring her out right away. I'll go find a small blanket." She turned to go do that.

"Mother?"

Looking over her shoulder, her expression remarkably sane, and seeming in complete control of herself, me, and the conversation, she said, "Yes, dear?"

"I'm sorry I snapped at you."

"I was a stupid old woman, not being more careful about that dosage. It won't happen again."

"I said you killed her, but really . . . you saved her." *After almost killing her. . . .*

Mother smiled sweetly. "Why, what would this place *be,* without our precious little guard dog?"

Dr. Tillie, a stocky, older man with a kind face and a gentle demeanor that had served him well, minimizing getting bit over the many years, had saved several of our pets' lives. Once upon a time, a twelve-year-old Brandy played a mean trick on Bluto, giving the bulldog a whole cooked turkey — seemed the dog had stolen the little girl's breakfast while she was off answering the phone — and Dr. Tillie had successfully pumped the dog's stomach. Then another time, Pippi, our one-eyed parrot (actually our only parrot, one-eyed or otherwise) got loose and attacked a rooster, and yet the ever-reliable vet managed to save her life, too.

Even though it was way past closing time for the animal hospital, Dr. Tillie — whose house was behind the kennels — was waiting for us just inside the unlocked door when we arrived. He took a cursory look at Sushi, who I held swaddled in a little pink blanket, and said, "Bring her in back."

We followed Dr. Tillie through the disinfectant-scented waiting room and then down a tiled hallway to one of several examination rooms. Here I placed Sushi-in-the-blanket on a gleaming steel table.

Sushi, conscious now, kept struggling vainly to stand on the cold, slippery surface, so I gently restrained her, as the vet listened to her heart, checked her eyes and mouth, then drew some blood for testing. She was frightened, and it broke my heart (the Prozac could only blunt so much emotion).

"Will she be all right?" I asked anxiously.

"I believe so," Dr. Tillie said. "But I'd like to keep her here under observation for at least twenty-four hours."

Still the picture of sanity, Mother asked, "Will there be someone checking on her through the night?"

Dr. Tillie nodded. "One of my nurses comes in twice to monitor the animals in intensive care, which is where I'll put Sushi." His smile was kind and there was nothing manufactured about it — he really cared. "We'll call you if there's any change."

I gave the vet my cell number, and Mother's, along with our home number, and thanked him for all he had done. I kissed Sushi, she granted me a lick on the nose, and then Mother and I left.

It was almost ten at night by the time we arrived back home, the house feeling cavernously empty without Sushi. Funny how such a small creature could fill up so big a space.

While Mother tidied up the mess she had made earlier in the kitchen, I made myself a bed on the uncomfortable Queen Anne needlepoint sofa, to be near the downstairs phone in case Dr. Tillie's nurse called.

Then Mother trundled upstairs to sleep, but not without saying what she used to say to a little Brandy while tucking me in: "Good night, sleep tight, don't let the bedbugs bite. If they do, take a shoe, and beat them till they're black and blue."

Did I ever mention I've had chronic nightmares since childhood?

I slept fitfully, waking several times imagining — not bed-bugs — but the sound of Sushi's little toenails clicking on the parquet floor. Once I even thought she was up on the couch with me, curled up in her usual spot in the crux of my bent knees, but the little lump was only a wad of blanket.

Finally, around four a.m., I drifted off into a deep sleep. I had several dreams, the last of which was at the flea market, where I walked endless aisles, spotting great bargains and going off to find Mother, only to bring her back to a table arrayed with completely different, unappealing, overpriced items. Joe Lange was in the dream, too, up ahead of me in the aisle — I would call out to him and he would walk faster,

127

pretending he hadn't heard me. Then someone gripped my shoulder and scared the
what's-it out of me . . .

. . . but it was only Mother, rubbing my
arm.

"Come along, dear," she said, "we must
act quickly."

The "act quickly" made me bolt upright.
"Is it Sushi? Is something wrong with —"

"No, dear," Mother interrupted sooth-
ingly, "the little darling is expected to make
a full and complete recovery. I just spoke
with Dr. Tillie, who says his patient is doing
spiffily. You may call him back if you like,
but he said we can pick her up at closing
time today."

My sigh of relief only made me realize that
my mouth tasted like an old gym sock —
not that I've ever tasted one. "Then why all
the excitement?" I asked.

Mother sat next to me on the sofa. "Important news has just come from my top-
secret contact within the police department. . . ."

I once asked Mother who this "top-secret
contact" was, but she refused to tell me,
claiming she didn't want me to be culpable.
But I was almost positive the PD leak was
Wanda, the night dispatcher, forever grate-
ful to Mother for helping land her a job as

an extra in *Field of Dreams;* unmarried Wanda kept her autographed photo from Kevin Costner on her desk where most people showed off family photos.

I tried looking at Mother straight on, but my neck was too stiff to turn, a hazzard from sleeping on the uncomfy couch. "And what news would that be?" I asked.

"My worst fears have come true! My darkest suspicions are bearing fruit!"

"What fears? What fruit?"

"Our poor little Chaz has been charged with her grandfather's murder!"

I swiveled to face Mother. "That's awful. You're sure?"

"My mole at the Police Department is utterly reliable."

Mother has more moles burrowed in and around town than the municipal golf course after a hard rain.

I asked, "What can we do to help her?"

Her chin jutted, her eyes narrowed. "Already *done,* dear."

"What's already done? *What* have you done, Mother?"

"Simply arranged the best possible counsel — Mr. Ekhardt himself has agreed to represent Chaz!"

Mr. Ekhardt was the most legendary criminal attorney Serenity had ever known;

but he was also just a shade older than the courthouse. His age, however, was not my foremost concern.

"Can he?" I asked. "I mean, can he represent a British citizen?"

"He can indeed," Mother said, adding, "And we certainly can't leave the poor girl's fate in the hands of a public defender!"

I could have. Some of the best lawyers in Serenity pitched in as public defenders; and the thought of the Borne girls winding up paying for Mr. Ekhardt's expensive services made a night of Mother shopping on Home Network seem a trifling matter.

Mother was saying, "We're to meet him at his office in one hour — sharp." She slapped my knee. "So, let's the two of us just hippity-hop to the barbershop!"

Okay, let's all of us agree that some old expressions need to die with our generation.

Mother rushing to call Mr. Ekhardt was no surprise, and not entirely because of his sterling reputation as a defense lawyer. Mr. Ekhardt had been our family lawyer since Peggy Sue was in diapers.

He'd skyrocketed to fame around here in the 1950s when — so the local lore goes — he got a woman off for murder after she shot her philandering husband four times.

In the back! (Accidentally, while cleaning her handgun.) No one believed her story, of course, but in a case that preceded by decades the Burning Bed and other cases of murdered abusive husbands, Ekhardt had introduced evidence showing the husband had regularly gone on drunken binges and beaten up his wife. Ekhardt had never offered this as mitigation for murder, sticking by his client's story. But the jury did what the jury had to do, and set her free.

Never before had the floral and candy shops in Serenity been so busy as after that trial's surprise outcome, worried husbands all over town rushing to appease their wives to prevent the same thing from happening to them.

The downtown sidewalks were shoveled and the city's Christmas decorations were up, a scratchy sound system worthy of a carnival barker ("Crazy Ball, Crazy Ball, come play the Crazy Ball!") somehow not defeating the various instrumental versions of the seasonal songs it bleated. Nothing religious, of course, just the likes of "Silver Bells" and "White Christmas." As Mother had once commented, "What would Christmas be without all that wonderful music written by Jewish tunesmiths!"

Mr. Ekhardt had an office on the top floor

of the Laurel Building, an eight-story Art Deco edifice (built 1928) on Main Street. At one time the successful trial attorney had owned the entire building, using all but the first floor for his flourishing practice. But as Ekhardt eased into semiretirement, he'd sold the building to an engineering firm with the stipulation that he be granted a lifetime lease of the eighth floor for a dollar a year. (Bet they never thought he'd reach eighty-eight!)

After finding a parking spot in front of the building, I hurriedly got out of the car so that I could beat Mother to the meter. Why? Because for some time now she had been depositing only slugs. (Mother had a long-running feud with the city council, trying to convince them to dispense with the meters, because nothing infuriates a shopper more than spending money downtown and receiving the warm thank-you note of a parking ticket.)

I shared Mother's sentiment, but her slugs invariably jammed the meters, and she would then leave a note saying that she had attempted to put coins into the "hungry maw of the meter, only to find it out of order, possibly by an Act of God." She had done this frequently enough that her getting busted over nickels and dimes seemed an inevitability.

We entered the refurbished lobby — Mother grousing about the loss of its antique fixtures (the building's loss, and ours, for not knowing they were going to be auctioned off) — then took the modern elevator up to the top floor.

Stepping off the elevator was like going back into time. While the rest of the floors had been modernized, the eighth floor retained its original style: scuffed black-and-white speckled ceramic-tiled floor, scarred-wood office doors with ancient pebbled glass, Art Moderne scone wall lighting, even an old porcelain drinking fountain.

Mr. Ekhardt — long since a one-man operation, reachable by appointment only — occupied the river-view corner office at the end of the long corridor. As we walked along, snoopy Mother tried the knob of each door on either side of the hallway, disappointed to find them all locked.

"Stop that," I said.

Mother shrugged. "Could be some incredible forgotten antiques in there, you know, just waiting to be discovered."

"Well, set sail on that expedition some other time, why don't you?"

We reached the last pebbled-glass door,

where stencils applied many decades ago now read:

Way e Ek ar t
Atto ney At La

Mother turned the round, worn brass knob.

"Locked, too." She frowned.

I checked my Chico's watch. We were right on time.

Mother and I exchanged puzzled looks.

"Do you think he's forgotten?" I asked.

As if in answer, the elevator dinged at the other end of the corridor.

"Ah, there the dear boy is," Mother said, beaming in satisfaction. "He hasn't lost his faculties yet."

Misplaced a few, maybe.

The elevator door whooshed open and the "boy," a frail-looking Mr. Ekhardt, stepped off. While his clothes looked dapper enough — charcoal wool topcoat, tan-and-red plaid scarf, black homburg — he seemed to have shrunk inside of them.

Mother and I watched silently as the lawyer shuffled slowly toward us. Remember Tim Conway's old man on the Carol Burnett TV Show, moving endlessly forward? Slower. (I could have painted my nails in the amount of time it took. Two coats.)

Finally, Mr. Ekhardt — somewhat winded from his long trip down the hallway, the bags under his eyes fully packed for a much-needed vacation — greeted us with a nod. Then, with shaky hands, he fished out keys on a chain, selected one, and unlocked the door and bade us enter in no more time than it took to write the first chapter of this book.

I was starting to seriously wonder if the legendary defense attorney was still up to the job of representing Chaz, and looked at Mother to see if she, too, had reservations. But Mother merely smiled back with utter confidence. The only reservations this woman had were at her favorite Serenity restaurant, the Woodfire Grill, for supper.

Mr. Ekhardt's small, sparse office came as something of a shock — the only things keeping this from passing for Phillip Marlowe's or Mike Hammer's digs was the lack of a sexy secretary. Was there a bottle of Scotch filed away in a desk drawer?

And where was the computer? Where were the law books? Or even a few dusty files on the well-worn desk, which was bare save for a solitary telephone? At least it wasn't a candlestick phone.

The lawyer, gesturing for us to be seated

in two oak captain's chairs opposite his desk, must have read my mind. "I conduct most of my work at home these days, Miss Borne," he explained. "I just maintain this office for show."

I managed a smile. "And what show would that be . . . *Peter Gunn*?"

The lawyer found that uproariously funny, but his laugh quickly turned into a hacking cough that weakened him further, and he dropped down into his swivel chair, gasping for breath.

Mother shot me a scolding glance, as if to say, "If our lawyer dies on us, young lady, it will be *your* fault!"

Mr. Ekhardt, exhausted, sighed and closed his eyes. I remembered Nero Wolfe in the Rex Stout novels Mother had insisted I read (one of her better recommendations); the corpulent sleuth would shut his eyes and do his best work as he became lost in thought. Perhaps Mr. Ekhardt was of that rare contemplative breed.

Only, in another moment, he was snoring.

Now I shot Mother a look, a withering, disenchanted one.

"We can afford to let him rest," Mother countered. "After all, he's not a young man anymore. He needs to conserve his energy, and marshal his enthusiasm."

Wondering if this were a rest or a coma, I trained my eyes on my watch and waited. After exactly two minutes and thirty-eight seconds, Mother gave a certifiably fake, "Ah . . . ah . . . ah . . . *choo!*"

And Mr. Ekhardt woke up with a snort. The attorney seemed startled to suddenly see us, but then most people are. It was just that most people who reacted that way hadn't minutes before invited us to sit down opposite them.

Mother leaned forward. "Wayne, what have your investigations told you thus far?"

He blinked. "What investigations?"

"Into this case."

"What case?"

"Why, *Chaz,* of course. The little Cockney street urchin accused of murder."

Did I detect a little tone of irritation in Mother's voice? And would I ever be able to banish the image in my mind of Chaz dressed like one of the ragamuffins in *Oliver?*

"Ah, yes." The lawyer nodded. "The British bird. That's what they call the British girls, you know — birds."

We waited.

"Well?" Mother asked. Apparently, she'd been hoping for more than the slang definition of "bird."

Mr. Ekhardt signed deeply, wearily. Something seemed to click into gear. "The evidence against the girl *is* formidable."

When he didn't elaborate, I asked, "Such as?"

"An envelope containing a small amount of potassium cyanide was found hidden under the girl's mattress. This, of course, is the same poison that killed Mr. Yeager."

I could tell by Mother's expression (smiling lips, frowning forehead) that she was conflicted: pleased that her theory of cyanide had been confirmed, upset to lose Chaz as an actress for the upcoming Christie.

"Furthermore," the attorney continued, "there's a little matter of the girl's prior conviction in England. . . ."

"Which," I stated, "wouldn't be admissible at trial, right?" Hey, I wasn't a complete novice; I'd seen *Law and Order.*

Ekhardt's nodding head was at odds with his words. "But a good trial lawyer could find a way to introduce it. And the county attorney is a good trial lawyer, as are his two deputies."

Mother sat forward, eyes batting behind the magnifying lenses. "Wayne — what was Chaz convicted of across the pond?"

The attorney's spindly eyebrows climbed

138

his wrinkled brow, then dropped, indicating that we weren't going to like what he had to say.

"Manslaughter."

Mother shrugged. "That's not so terrible."

The man getting slaughtered might disagree — assuming he could.

I asked, "What happened?"

Ekhardt said, "Seems she fed her stepfather poisoned mushrooms."

Rut-row.

Mother pshawed, "An honest mistake — one mushroom pretty much looks much like another."

Which is why I never eat any mushrooms Mother picks, and advise you to do the same.

Ekhardt sighed, "Except the girl *did* plead guilty to the lesser charge."

"Oh, dear," Mother said, reality finally poking through.

"So what happens next?" I asked.

The lawyer leaned back in his well-worn leather chair. "The arraignment is tomorrow afternoon at three."

"Should we be there?" I asked, which was a silly question — nothing short of a court order could have kept Mother away, and I'm not sure they issue restraining orders to make you stay so many feet away from a courthouse — although it's probably come up for discussion in Serenity where Mother is concerned.

Ekhardt said simply, "I'm sure our young lady would appreciate the support."

Then he folded his hands across his stomach and closed his eyes, which I took as our dismissal and not Nero Wolfean contemplation.

"Well, thank you, Wayne," Mother said, rising.

I got up, too, and my chair scraped the floor.

Ekhardt's eyelids fluttered open. "There *is* one other thing. The young woman spoke about a missing book. . . ."

Mother and I exchanged startled expressions.

"The Tarzan book is *missing?*" Mother asked.

"If that indeed is what the girl was referring to, then, yes. The book is gone. I understand it's quite valuable."

Then his eyes closed again, and the soft snoring resumed.

We gathered our raccoon coats and tiptoed out of the office, quietly shutting the pebbled-glass door behind us.

"Finally!" Mother said in a loud whisper. "A development!"

I didn't bothering whispering. "By that, you mean finally we have a murder motive."

Now was not the time to share my secret with Mother: namely, that my friend Joe Lange had harbored a desire for the very book that was now missing, possibly/ probably stolen. . . .

Mother was moving quickly down the corridor, for a woman who'd had a hip replacement. "A murder motive indeed! If that Tarzan book *has* been purloined, it means that Chaz did *not* kill her grandfather."

"Maybe she was *lying* about it being stolen," I said, trying to keep up; my hips were younger than her remaining old one, but that new one of hers was still a threat. "And it's hidden away somewhere."

Mother halted, and I bumped into her.

"And why would the dear child do that?" she asked, whirling, her eyes wide behind the big glasses.

"To avert suspicion from herself, of course."

She turned and started walking again. "Nonsense! You know full well the murderer is that *book* scout. . . . What did you say his name was? Harry Potthoff. *He* paid Walter a visit on that fateful morning, and when he and Walter couldn't come to terms on the sale of the book, well, that scoundrel simply slipped cyanide in Walter's coffee."

I shook my head. "Pudgy may be a scoundrel . . . but a murderer? Besides, he's way too obvious. . . . Would never happen in a Perry Mason."

Of course, Perry Mason would never fall asleep in the middle of a consultation.

Mother put her hands on her hips, new and old. "All right then, Little Miss Smartypants, who do you think *did* do it?"

I frowned in thought. "Why not suicide?"

"*What?* Why, that's utterly ridiculous! Explain."

We were at the elevator now.

"Think about it," I said, "Mr. Yeager's health was failing. He realized that what little money he had left — money he wanted to go to Chaz — would get gradually eaten away by medical bills. Or maybe not so gradually. Anyway, that morning, while Chaz was at her boyfriend's, Yeager swallowed cyanide, believing his death would be blamed on another heart attack."

Mother seemed skeptical. "And the Tarzan novel?"

I pushed the button to summon the elevator. "Well, obviously, Yeager *did* sell it to someone, and somewhere there's got to be proof of that."

Mother raised a forefinger. "Or perhaps

Chaz sold the book, and is afraid to mention it because it would look like a good *murder* motive!"

"Which," I said glumly, "it is."

Our ride arrived and we stepped onto an empty elevator. But it was slow going down, the elevator stopping on every floor, filling up with employees heading out for lunch, and soon Mother and I were the two sardines pushed farthest back in the corner of the can.

Mother, quiet until now, blurted, "I *still* think the book scout killed him!"

A dozen or so pair of eyes looked our way, and I smiled back with a nervous laugh. "Audio book we're listening to. Agatha Christie? *Murder Is Easy?*"

Mother tsk-tsked. "And what a *horrible* way to die! One might think swallowing cyanide is relatively painless, but the horrible reality is something otherwise. . . ."

I tried pinching Mother, but couldn't get my fingers through her thick girdle.

". . . first your heart stops, then your face turns *purple* and your eyes *bulge* out —"

I stepped on Mother's shoe and her eyes bulged out as she went *"Yowwww!"* particularly loud, because that was the foot with the corn.

The elevator door whooshed open, revealing the lobby, and everyone around us scurried off like *Titanic* passengers looking for a lifeboat.

Mother, hobbling off the elevator, asked crossly, "Was that really necessary?"

"Was describing the effects of cyanide poisoning really necessary?"

Mother grunted, but made no other protest or defense.

Outside, a ticket thumbed its nose at us from the windshield of my poor defenseless car.

"Oh, come *on!*" I said. "We weren't in there *that* long!"

Mother smiled triumphantly. "Perhaps in the future this will teach you to allow *me* to handle the parking meter problem, dear."

"From now on," I said disgustedly, "it's all yours," grabbing the yellow ticket off.

Want to hear something *completely* despicable? Some cities have installed so-called "smart" parking meters that sense when a car vacates its space, and if there's any time left on the meter, it resets itself! How petty can you get?

I'm with Mother; bring on the slugs.

This was the first chance we'd had to restock our booth with our flea market finds, and with Christmas fast approaching, the holiday items we'd scored had a short shelf life — specifically a set of bubble lights from the 1940s (with questionable wiring that I hoped wouldn't set some buyer's real tree on fire), a 1950s bank of a sleeping Santa in an easy chair, and a set of four wax candle carolers.

With the help of Red Feather, my Indian spirit guide — who is good at getting me parking places, but whose magical powers apparently do not extend to avoiding expired meters — I managed to nab a free thirty-minute loading zone spot in front of the downtown antiques mall. Which almost made up for the earlier ticket.

Almost.

I retrieved our box of collectibles from the back of the car, and we entered the Victorian, turn-of-the-last-century brick building with its ornate facade and unique corner-set front door.

The old four-story structure had a checkered past, several former owners having died under unusual circumstances; but the new owner, Raymond Spillman, had had the building blessed by a priest before moving in — Mother insisted a "reliable source" had told her a full-scale exorcism had been performed — and so far, so good.

Ray — as everyone called him — was a small, spry man in his late seventies, with a slender build, thinning gray hair, bright shining eyes, bulbous nose, and a slash of a mouth. Mother claimed he'd graduated from high school with her, but since Mother keeps adjusting her age downward, it was becoming increasingly hard to find anyone over sixty-five who hadn't been in her (nonspecified) graduating class. (Mother attends all class reunions from 1941 through 1948.)

At the moment, there were few customers in the vast antiques mall, perhaps due to the lunch hour, but Ray — a former sewing machine salesman — was busy, nonetheless, at the center circular checkout station. He was working on an antiquated Singer with its parts laid out neatly on the counter, a surgeon preparing to put back the innards of a patient.

According to Mother (who would share with me all sorts of worthless information when I was a captive audience stuck behind the wheel of the car), Ray had once been a womanizer and a "drunkard," but when his first grandchild was born, he turned into a dry model citizen.

Look, if I have to listen to her worthless information, so do you.

Mother chirped, "Good afternoon, Ray . . . aren't you looking fit as a fiddle! Have you been taking some kind of youth serum?"

Mother always laid it on thick with the widower, hoping not to spike romantic interest, but in search of a bigger dealer discount.

Ray's cheeks turned as red as Santa Claus's suit. "Oh, Vi-Vivian . . . hell-hello."

Mother continued. "Come now, Ray, *admit* it! You could pass for sixty. . . . Couldn't he pass for sixty, Brandy?"

I hated it when she pulled me into her blarney, so instead I asked, "How are Mother and I doing this month, Ray?"

Meaning, sales in our booth. I was counting on a good payday to cover all my Christmas charges, and avoid the stiff interest rates.

Ray smiled, showing stained teeth, a byproduct of the ever-present bottle of Cola-Cola always within his reach; one was on the counter right now.

"Everyone's having a record month!" he relayed happily.

Mother beamed and so did I. "How wonderful!" she replied. Then, innocently, she added, "Could I take the teensy-weensiest peek at the ledger book?"

Ray didn't use a computer, keeping track of sales by hand. But his wary expression said he saw through Mother's apparently offhand request.

First of all, Mother never "peeked" at anything — especially our page in the accounts payable register. She studied, analyzed, dissected, and agonizingly scrutinized, but peeked? No.

And second, she was breaking protocol by asking to see how much Ray owed us before we'd restocked and straightened our booth. It was kind of like asking your parents for an advance on your next week's allowance when you haven't cleaned your room this week.

But Ray complied with Mother's request, reaching under the counter and producing his oversized accounts book, which he placed on the glass top, making room among the sewing machine parts and his current Coke bottle.

I had been holding the heavy box all this time, and so I finally set it down, to be able to peer over Mother's shoulder as she quickly leafed through the register to locate our page.

The long list of antiques and collectibles that we had sold so far this month brought a grin to my face — half of the money being mine — so Mother's reaction took me by surprise.

She blurted, "Shit!"

Then she added, "Shit, shit, shit!"

Mother doesn't swear or curse lightly, but the above does represent her expletive of choice.

A lone female browser who had just come through the end of a nearby aisle gave us a dirty look.

I hissed at Mother. "Shhhhhh!"

She glared back defiantly and said, "Shhhhh-*it!*"

"What's the *matter* with you? Can't you see how much we've sold?"

"To other *dealers!*" Mother snapped.

I stared at the page.

She was correct: nearly every item had a dealer discount deducted from our original price, in addition to the percentage that Ray took.

Mother seemed more upset than mad. "That means we've been underpricing!"

Which was a seller's conundrum. Should you price low enough for an immediate return on your investment, or price high and risk the item possibly never selling? (Splitting the difference didn't seem to occur to Mother.)

"Oh, look," I said, pointing to a line on our page, "the smiley-face clock finally sold!"

The kitschy bedside collectable had been

with us for over a year, an impulse garage sale purchase by yours truly, for which I'd paid way too much. Mother had grown tired of seeing the grinning clock in our booth month after month, that smile a seemingly gleeful reminder of her daughter's misstep, and we'd set about to rid ourselves of the thing, trying everything from shining a spotlight on its face to featuring the clock on a fancy doily.

We'd even placed it precariously on the edge of a table so some poor browser might knock it off to the floor, bringing "you break it you bought it" into play. (I did not approve of this last sales tactic of Mother's.) (But desperate times require desperate measures.)

Mother smirked. "The clock *did* sell, all right . . . to a *dealer!*"

I couldn't win.

Sighing, I bent and picked up our box of restock, then headed to our booth, which was nicely positioned to the right of the front door entrance (and which no other dealer had wanted because it was number thirteen — the Borne girls flying in the face of adversity and superstition).

Mother soon joined me, and we went through our usual routine: I unpacked and dusted the items; she positioned and tagged them. After I'd finished my tasks, I went back to talk to Ray, but found him engrossed again with the sewing machine, so I decided not to bother him.

The accounts book remained out on the counter, however, and I began leafing through it, to see how we had fared compared to the other dealers. Behind the counter, a vintage eight-track tape player was emitting Christmas tunes, with the Andrews Sisters doing "Winter Wonderland" only to be interrupted halfway and midphrase by the weird eight-track channel changing.

Booth twelve, next to ours, and rented by Mr. Beatty, appeared to be the top moneymaker this month; he stocked old comic books and collectable toys, the latter bringing in good sales at Christmas.

The Deasons, booth three, featuring mostly glassware, had a big run on Jadite Fireking dishes, putting them in the second spot. (Have you ever dropped one of those? Wow, talk about a thousand little pieces. . . .)

Then I noticed a new renter in booth five, with a familiar moniker: Harry Potthoff. His page was nearly blank, save for the sale of a few inexpensive books.

Interrupting Ray, I said, "This Mr. Potthoff . . . when did he start renting?"

Without looking up from his work, Ray answered, "Beginning of the month."

"Hasn't sold much," I noted idly. "Bad location?"

Mother and I had turned down that booth opposite the badly ventilated bathroom, taking our chances with our unlucky number.

Now Ray looked up. "Prices too high."

"Then how does he make any money?"

The old gent shrugged. "I don't ask . . . as long as he pays his rent on time."

I shrugged. "Maybe he has money, and this is a hobby with him."

Ray shook his head. "Said he was a retired teacher."

"Wealthy wife?"

"Not married."

"Girlfriend?"

Ray had close to an irritated look on his usually placid face. I was interrupting his work.

Oh, well, what did I care *where* Pudgy got the hard cash for the expensive David Yurman watch? Or who he was giving it to?

But Mother would.

A TRASH 'N' TREASURES TIP

When spending the day at a flea market, go prepared. Wear comfortable shoes and layers of clothing that can be shed. Bring an umbrella for rain, and protective lotion for sun. Pack water and snacks, aspirin and Band-Aids. It's a jungle out there.

CHAPTER SIX:
KEEP YOUR
SUNNY-SIDE UP

I had been inside the secondary courtroom of the Serenity Courthouse several times, thanks to various traffic violations Mother had racked up over the past few years. (As of now, Mother will not be eligible to drive again until the ripe old age of one hundred and nine, a birthday she has every intention of reaching, by which time, with any luck, the planet will have run out of fossil fuels.)

In the mornings, this room was used for traffic court, when herds of ensnared citizens were processed in a quick, noisy cattle call to justice. Afternoons, however, were reserved for felony arraignments, and the atmosphere was strikingly different: quiet, somber, and depressing, perhaps in part due to the loss of the morning sunlight.

At the moment, the only people waiting for Chaz's arraignment to begin were Mother, myself, Mr. Ekhardt, and Chaz's boyfriend, Ben Adams. We were seated in the right front pew, with the county attorney across the aisle, a middle-aged man in a dark gray tailored suit — no off-the-rack stuff for our CA, who had family money that could see to it his frame was properly draped, and that was good, because he was fond of eating and the resultant shape was unlikely to be found on any rack, outside of a Big, Tall, and Weirdly Bulging men's store.

I won't go into what the rest of us were wearing, except for Ben, seated next to me, because he looked so radically different than the scruffy young tough who'd run past me the night of the flea market preshow. To show support for Chaz, he'd gone all the way: a navy suit, a black necktie, his dark hair neatly combed, slender face free from stubble. You'd think *he* were the accused, trying to make a good first impression on the judge, who had yet to arrive.

I whispered to Ben, "It'll be fine," although I was in no way sure it would be. "Mr. Ekhardt's a legend."

Ben turned his worried eyes to me. "What, like Bigfoot? Get a load of the old geezer." He gestured with his head toward the celebrated attorney. "He's asleep!"

I looked down our row, where, on the other side of Mother, our frail-looking local Perry Mason snored softly, his chin resting on his pin-stripped vest. I would have yelled, "Boo!" if I hadn't been afraid it would give him a coronary.

The CA seemed to have overheard Ben's harsh remark, and he made a smug *harrumph.*

Which Mother overheard.

She leaned forward, turned her critical eyes toward Jabba the County Attorney, and sneered. "Wipe that smirk off your face, young man. . . . You're not worthy of carrying Wayne Ekhardt's sweaty jockstrap out of the gym!"

Well, folks, that was by and large the most startling thing Mother had ever said in a courtroom, and I'd heard her say plenty of shocking things before. Her comment conjured up two very disturbing images for me: scrawny senior citizen Mr. Ekhardt in a sweaty jockstrap; and the corpulent CA in gym shorts tiptoeing out the door carrying said strap by a dainty thumb and middle finger.

The CA smirked again, but before Mother could retaliate, I touched her arm. "Let's not make an even bigger enemy out of him, Mother."

"Could we have a 'bigger' enemy?" she asked.

Good point.

But amazingly, Mother heeded my advice. "Still, dear, you're quite right — one should be respectful in a court of law."

"You're doing fine so far," I said.

Mother reared back. "When have I *ever* behaved in a manner less than dignified in a serious situation such as this?"

"You want them chronologically, or in alphabetical order?"

While we were waiting, an unsettling thought came to me: Young Ben had spruced himself up for Chaz today, just as he'd stolen that flea market money bag for her the other night. What else might he have done for Chaz? Kill her grandfather?

The side door next to the judge's bench swung open, commanding our attention, and a beefy male bailiff strode in, taking his place next to the standing American flag, hands fig-leafed before him.

I had been expecting, even hoping for, the sadistic, gum-chewing lady from traffic court for a little comic relief; but apparently, for felony arraignments, a more formidable bailiff was required. Any comic relief would have to be handled by Mother, which was enough to make me plead "Guilty!" and I wasn't even accused of anything.

Next, a female judge entered, black robe flapping, and Mother made an audible sound of approval, seeing who was going to be running the show. I, too, recognized the middle-aged African American woman from Mother's last traffic court appearance, where Mother had launched into an impromptu monologue to defend herself, and the judge became so irritated and outraged that she banged the gavel down on her thumb.

The judge took her place behind the raised bench, gazed out toward the gallery, her eyes widening as she spotted Mother in the front row, smiling and waving. Fortunately, Mother stopped just short of yelling, "Yoo hoo!" but she did chirp, "Hello, Judge Jones . . . remember me from traffic court? I do hope your thumb is back to its normal size."

Judge Jones's mouth didn't say anything, but the rest of her face spoke volumes; it would be a long time indeed before she'd ever forget Mother.

The side door opened for the third time and a female ponytailed deputy ushered in a handcuffed Chaz, who was almost unrecognizable in a plain gray woolen dress — its high neckline covering her barbed-wire tattoo — black pumps, her black hair in soft curls, face scrubbed clean of makeup, the various piercing hardware absent.

Chaz's eyes darted furtively from Ben to me to Mother, then took on alarm at the still-snoozing Mr. Ekhardt.

"Oy!" she said. "Your Honor, I want me a new solicitor! One that's alive, yeah?"

The burly bailiff bellowed, "Quiet! This court is now in session, the Honorable Judge Jones presiding."

The judge banged her gavel, and then, and only then, did Ekhardt's eyes snap open, his body flexing, suddenly energized, a race-horse put out to pasture but still responding to the sound of the starting gun. He rose from the pew, tottering only slightly, and joined his client in front of the bench.

I knew from experience that arraignments were quick, the process being limited to a "guilty" or "not guilty" plea (Mother always pleaded "nolo contendere" just to be ornery). So I expected to be out on the street in no time.

Judge Jones looked at her notes, then said, "The State versus Charlotte Doxley. Does the defendant have representation?"

"Yes, Your Honor," Ekhardt said in a surprisingly commanding voice.

"For the record," the judge noted, "Wayne Ekhardt is representing the defendant."

I forgot to mention the court reporter in the corner, a woman with mousy brown hair and dark circles under her eyes, seated at her little machine, fingers flying, providing a faint percussive clicking in the background.

The judge looked at Chaz. "You are Charlotte Doxley?"

"Yes, mum," Chaz responded weakly.

"You understand the process of this arraignment?"

"I guess I do."

"Well, do you or don't you?" the judge asked impatiently.

"Yeah, I do. Mum."

Satisfied, Judge Jones stated, "You are charged with felony murder. How do you plead?"

Everyone waited for the expected "not guilty" from Ekhardt, who would speak for his client, but the words that he uttered were surprising.

"Your Honor," the lawyer said measuredly, "I request a motion for dismissal of this charge against my client on the grounds that the search warrant was improperly issued — specifically it was issued *after* the officers entered the mobile home of Walter Yeager, making all evidence obtained on the premises at that time inadmissible."

One could have heard the proverbial pin drop. Or a real one, for that matter.

The smug county attorney leapt to his feet in a flurry of fat. "Your Honor! I protest! Any objection to that search warrant is purely a matter of semantics, the warrant itself a mere formality, the victim being the sole owner of the mobile home!"

The judge addressed Ekhardt, her eyes narrowed. "You have a copy of the warrant?"

Ekhardt nodded. "*And* the detective's report, which clearly indicates that the home was entered a full hour before the warrant was issued."

The CA began to stutter. "A-a-again I protest, Your Honor — a search warrant was not strictly necessary for the home of the murder victim."

"I disagree," Ekhardt said. He held up another paper. "Mr. Yeager may have lived on those premises, but he was not the 'sole owner,' in fact not the owner at all. This is a copy of the transfer of title of that mobile home into the name of Charlotte Doxley — filed ten days *before* Mr. Yeager's death. Miss Doxley should have been served with a warrant to search her *own* property. Therefore, I ask once again that this charge against my client be dropped, and she be released immediately."

I said, "Wow!"

Mother said, "Hot damn!"

Chaz said, "Crikey!"

Ben said, "Yes!"

The CA didn't say anything, although his mouth hung open as if he hoped some higher power would see fit to send some words on through.

"*Order!*" Judge Jones banged the gavel. Carefully. "Mr. Ekhardt, I'd like to see that title."

The judge studied the document for a moment, brow furrowed, then shot the county attorney a reproachful look.

The gavel banged again, and the judge said, "The charges against Charlotte Doxley are dismissed." She gathered her papers from the bench, and then swished out the side door, her robe waving good-bye. Or maybe good riddance.

Chaz turned to Ekhardt. "Is it true? I can *go?*"

Ekhardt, smiling sagely, just nodded.

She gave the lawyer a big bear hug, which he seemed to enjoy, despite the sounds of bones popping.

The CA walked over to our stunned but happy little group, now crowded around Chaz, and said tersely to the defendant, "Congratulations, Miss Doxley . . . but my advice to you is not to go too far. We do have extradition agreements with Great Britain."

And he tromped out of the courtroom, making minor earthquakes as he went.

Ben asked Ekhardt, "What did he mean by that?"

Ekhardt sighed. "He means he intends almost certainly to bring new charges against Miss Dockley. I'm afraid this isn't over yet. . . ."

Mother frowned. "How is that possible? This is America! What about double jeopardy?"

"It's not applicable, Vivian," Ekhardt said, "because we haven't gone to trial. An arraignment doesn't set the double-jeopardy exception into motion."

Chaz's face was screwed up with worry. "Wha' should I *do* then, Mr. Ekhardt?"

The lawyer spread his slender arms out to encompass his small flock. "Let's continue this discussion outside, shall we?"

A few minutes later, we gathered on the courthouse steps under a gunmetal gray winter sky. The distorted sounds of instrumental carols being bleated over cheap speakers, in the nearby downtown, provided a less-than-festive soundtrack. Ekhardt stood on the step above Chaz and Ben, like a preacher getting about to marry them, with Mother and me as bridesmaids below.

The lawyer looked at Ben. "Young man, do you have a relative or friend living out of state where Chaz could stay for a while? Just nod your head."

Ben, puzzled, nodded.

Ekhardt continued. "Too bad I can't suggest she go there, out of reach of local police. But that would be unethical — unlawful even — so I can't do so."

Chaz frowned. "Okay, guv . . . so I *won't,* then, yeah?"

But Ben smiled, following Ekhardt perfectly. Mother did, too, her big eyes behind the glasses dancing with delight at the strategy of this sly old fox, and she said lightly to Chaz, "Have a safe trip, my dear!"

Inside my head, I was going, "La la la la la la la la la," not wanting to be even an indirect party to circumventing the law. And I kept my own, probably unfair, suspicions about Ben to myself.

The next day, Saturday, I was down for the count with a migraine that wouldn't let go even after several doses of my headache medication. I wasn't sure why it came on: wrong food, hormones, stress, not enough sleep, too much sleep. . . . or maybe, yes, feeling guilty about being party to circumventing the law, encouraging two murder suspects to run off into hiding together.

But I *was* sure that Sushi had played a part, perhaps even praying to her shih tzu god for me to be put out of commission so she could stay in bed with me all day. While the little mutt snoozed peacefully on top of the covers, I had delirious dreams about going to jail for helping keep Chaz out of jail.

I was supposed to go out with Brian — it was his night off — with dinner and movie on the docket, but I had to call and leave word on his answer machine that a migraine had taken me out of the game. I tried to sound as sweet as I could, since the last time we'd spoken (at that mobile home) had been strained, and I didn't want him to read anything into what was a genuinely migraine-motivated cancellation.

Mother knew enough to leave me alone in my darkened room for the duration, but about dinnertime, she tiptoed in.

"Brandy, dear, I asked my Red-Hatted League ladies to scour the town for Popsicles . . . and Frannie, bless her heart, found some . . . which, in the wintertime, is like finding Easter eggs in the fall."

I slowly sat up, eyes trying to focus on what Mother held out in her hand. Sometimes a cold treat *could* chase my migraine away at the end of its cycle. . . .

"What flavor?"

"Grape. And not to worry! I washed off the freezer-burn."

Purple was not my favorite flavor, but I stuck the Popsicle in my mouth anyway, and even though it still smacked of the inside wall of a freezer, I couldn't remember anything ever tasting so good.

I went though the whole box before the night was over.

Around nine, Mother came up and nudged me awake. "Your friend Brian's here, Brandy, checking up on you! Shall I shoo him away?"

"No! No. . . . Tell him I'll be right down."

I *was* feeling better. The headache had subsided, but I was left with an all-over sluggishness that prevented me from suggesting Brian and I catch the late show or something.

I bundled myself in a plaid woolen robe and slipped into slippers, taking a brief side trip to the bathroom to brush my teeth and gargle. I even brushed my hair a little, but didn't bother with makeup. That would have been a lost cause.

Anyway, Brian had seen me in my migraine state any number of times, and I was secretly glad to be able to show him I hadn't been faking.

My sandy-haired fella stood from where he'd been sitting on the sofa as I came down the staircase. I came over and gave him a little kiss, and we sat.

"I was worried about you," he said. He was in a sweatshirt and jeans, and I admit it was a relief not seeing him in his blue uniform.

"Mother said you were checking up on me."

"She doesn't like me much, does she?"

"I think she likes me unattached."

"Because your marriage *bruised* you or . . . ?"

"No. She doesn't want to lose her driver."

That made him smile. His puppy-dog brown eyes were troubled, though. "You okay?"

"It's beaten back," I said, referring to the migraine monster, a beast Brian knew all about. "Sorry about tonight."

"No problem. Listen . . . I just wanted to say, I hope you and your mother will just stay out of this Yeager mess. I heard you were at the arraignment."

"That was dropped. The judge set her free."

"Right, on a technicality. She's still our best suspect, and I don't trust that boy friend of hers, either. That's who stole that money you returned, right?"

"I plead the Fifth."

"Brandy, I'm asking you not as a cop, but as your friend."

"Oh, we're friends now?"

"Please stay out of this. That Chaz and Ben, they're a bad pair. But if you do talk to Chaz? Tell her not even to *think* about skipping town."

I folded my arms and stared at him. He didn't seem as cute to me suddenly. "Well, I can't begin to tell you how nice it is that you dropped by to see how I was feeling. But if you don't mind, I think my migraine just crawled back out of its cave."

"Brandy, I just . . ."

"We'll talk when I'm feeling better."

I walked him to the door, and he made a little move to kiss me, but I gave him a frozen smile and kind of, well, pushed him out and shut the door on him.

He had his nerve.

But then so did I, not telling him about Joe Lange. . . .

Sunday morning arrived, and even though I had slept for thirty-six hours, I still felt tired — if headache-free — when Mother traipsed in about nine o'clock in her house robe.

"And how are *we* today?" she asked.

I didn't know how she was, but I felt okay, and told her so.

Mother said cheerily, "Good! Church is in an hour." And she traipsed back out before I could protest.

Since she had gotten me those Popsicles, I guessed I could go along with her on this. So I sighed and headed for the shower.

A little backstory about how we landed at New Hope Church might be called for. Throughout much of my childhood, Mother and I would visit various churches in town, Mother looking for just the right heavenly fit for us earthly creatures. I do believe we tried them all: Presbyterian, Methodist, Episcopalian, Baptist, Lutheran, Catholic, Jehovah's Witness, and Mormon. We even went to synagogue (and, after a potluck dinner, we were ready to convert to Judaism for the matzoh ball soup alone).

Then Mother heard about Pastor John Tutor, who — when informed by his church elders that he would have to uproot his wife and two kids for a pulpit in another state — told those same powers-that-be to stick it. (In more Christian terms, I'm sure — send thy wishes to a holy place, maybe?) Anyway, Pastor Tutor resigned from said church, and formed a new one, taking half his old congregation with him.

For almost a month now, regular services at our church — located in a reconverted old fire station — had been suspended, ever since an ancient boiler had broken down and been deemed unrepairable, and a whole new heating system had had to be installed. Pastor Tutor, rather than close down the church for the duration of this upgrade, concocted a rather interesting, if unconventional, way of keeping his flock from wandering away to some other shepherd.

Remember the "flash mob" fad of a few years back? When text messaging on cell phones was a new phenomenon? People would contact their friends to meet at a certain place, and at a certain time, and then create a sudden crowd on a street corner (or wherever), only to disappear and confound everyone else in the immediate area.

Cell phone owners have, thankfully, found better uses for text messaging these days, but the prank did inspire Pastor Tutor to try something similar . . . however, our "flash mob" performs a not-so-random act of kindness, aiming to accomplish a good work before we disappear . . . supposedly.

I say "supposedly" because the first time we tried this, it was an unmitigated disaster

— thanks, of course, to Mother. She had heard through one of her various, overripened grapevines that a widowed member of the church (name withheld) wanted her living room remodeled, but couldn't afford it.

Taking a cue from the BBC show *While You Were Out,* our congregation swooped in when Mrs. Name Withheld was away for a weekend, and repainted and recovered and rearranged the room. Well, when Mrs. N.W. returned and saw what we had done, she threatened to sue the church unless "every last stick" was put back just the way it was! (My theory is that she specifically didn't care for the red-and-orange color scheme.) Anyway, since then, Pastor Tudor has always cleared whatever "good deed" we're about to do beforehand with the owner or proprietor in question.

This morning the cell phone–savvy members of our church got this text message: Plz B at Suny Sde Up, 10, wk clths, pnt brshs, CUL8R, Pstr Tutr. Meanwhile, the e-mail-educated got: Please be at Sunny Side Up Nursing Home at 10 am. Wear work clothes and bring paint brushes. See you later. Pastor Tutor, ☺ And finally, the computer illiterate (mostly older folks) received a personal phone call from the pastor with even more detailed information, plus an offer of a ride if need be.

A quick sidebar about Sunny Side Up.

The nursing home made the national news about ten years ago when a crackhead held the staff and elderly residents hostage at gunpoint, demanding money that none of them had. But what this home-grown terrorist didn't realize was that Sunny Side Up had recently taken in transfers from a nearby veterans' home, and I mean, these were ex-combat soldiers who'd been in the Battle of the Bulge, and fought at Bloody-Nose Ridge, and survived the beaches of Normandy! Well, those grizzled, old veterans dispatched that crackhead in short order, beginning with a crack on the head with a crutch, followed by a wallop in the groin with a walker, ending with a busted kneecap by a bedpan.

End of sidebar.

On this particular morning, we were giving the recreation room at the nursing home a fresh coat of paint (color *approved* by management), so after feeding Sushi and giving her some insulin, I wolfed down a plate of boysenberry pancakes. Then Mother and I donned our Jackson Pollock–splattered paint clothes, threw on our raccoon coats, and headed out to the Buick, each carrying a few old brushes whose bristles were stiff with dried paint.

The weather was sunny and surprisingly warm for December; most of the snow was melting, and it made for sloppy driving as we headed out Cedar Street to the nursing home, located just this side of the treacherous bypass (good call).

Sunny Side, housing about fifty residents, a modern, single-floor building with white siding, was designed in a U-shape, with a courtyard in the center. What with the usual Sunday visitors, plus the onslaught of New Hope Samaritans, the parking lot was full. I dropped Mother off at the entrance, then parked on an adjacent street and tromped back in the slush.

When I arrived in the lobby of the nursing home, some commotion was already going on in the recreation room, and we hadn't even started painting yet. It seemed — according to one henna-haired lady supported by a walker — that many of the residents were none too happy about being thrown out of their common room, depriving them of their normal Sunday morning activities.

But Pastor Tutor handled the crisis with his usual aplomb, assuring the unhappy ones we would be finished in an hour, at which time they could return to the big-screen TV, and checkers, and whatever else they did in there to occupy their time.

Then Pastor Tutor gathered his flock around — thirty or forty of us sheep — and led us in the Lord's Prayer, which was followed by a minute of silent prayer. (My personal plea to the Almighty? That we *would* finish painting in an hour. . . .)

What happened next is a sad commentary on the overrated intelligence of the human race, throwing into question how we got to the top of the food chain in the first place. Complete and utter chaos ensued as everyone tried to organize how to proceed with the painting.

Except me — I stood to one side, waiting for the dust to settle, and that was when I noticed that someone else was absent, someone who was usually in the thick of the fray: *Mother.*

I set my paintbrush down and began the hunt.

For the next ten minutes, I wandered the antiseptic-smelling hallways, peering into the open rooms — where sometimes the hospital beds were occupied, and other times not — and listening at the doors that were shut.

Finally, I heard Mother's voice coming from behind a closed door that bore, in a

little tag holder, the name GRACE CRAW-
FORD.

I pushed the door slowly inward and saw
Mother standing next to the slightly raised
bed, in which the elderly, frail-looking
Grace was propped, her shoulder-length
white hair splayed on the pillow.

Mother was saying, "My favorite Bible
verse is, 'There but for the grace of God go
I.' "

Which was weird in a number of ways,
starting with the other woman's name being
Grace.

Obviously, Mother would rather pontifi-
cate than paint.

Grace responded in a feeble voice, "*Mine*
is, 'Do unto others as they do unto you.' "

"Don't you mean, 'As *you would have them*
do unto you'?" Mother corrected. Then she
spotted me in the doorway. "Ah, Brandy,
come meet a dear old friend of mine. . . ."

Now, Mother had at least five hundred
"dear old friends," as her Christmas card
list attested to, so I was bound to run into a
few I hadn't met.

I joined Mother beside the bed. Grace's
frail body seemed skeletal beneath the covers, but her blue eyes were surprisingly
bright.

Grace said, "So this is your lovely daughter. . . ." She held out a bony hand, which I clasped.

"Hello, Grace," I said.

The woman looked at Mother with a yearning expression. "You were so lucky to have another child so late in life."

Wasn't she, I thought with a bitterness at odds with doing good works. *A miracle, even.*

Mother turned to me. "Grace's daughter and I were in high school together — she was a year ahead of me."

As I mentioned before, who wasn't?

"Oh, that's nice," I said. "Where's your daughter now, Grace?"

Sadness dimmed the blue eyes. "Gone, I'm afraid. Dead these many years."

"Oh, I'm sorry," I said quickly, then made things worse by following with, "Do you have any other children?"

The woman sighed. "No. Ella Jane was my only child."

I gave Mother a "thanks for getting me into this" look, but to her credit, she said, "Well, we must be get back to our painting."

As if Mother had ever begun!

To me, Grace said gracefully, "It was nice to meet you, Brandy."

I muttered the same; then Mother and I left, closing the door behind us.

As we walked down the hallway, toward the recreation room, I said to Mother, "Why do I think that the reason our church came here today was so that *you* could see that particular old lady?"

Mother scoffed, "Why, that's absurd, dear. . . . You have a devious mind."

"Runs in the family. What was that about, anyway?"

"It was about doing the Christian thing and visiting an old friend, when I noticed her name on the roster of residents here. My visit with Grace was *strictly* unintentional."

I smirked. "You never do anything unintentional, except maybe get me in hot water."

Mother merely smiled.

I asked, "So what happened to her daughter?"

Mother shook her head and did her tsk-tsk number. "A month after the girl went off to college, she hung herself — or is it hanged? I'm never certain of the usage."

I had stopped short in the hall. "*What? Why?*"

Mother also halted, and faced me. "The rumor back then was that poor Ella Jane discovered she was pregnant. And in those days . . . well, my dear . . . there weren't as

177

many options open for an unmarried woman."

Mother walked on, but I stayed put, thinking about the better option Peggy Sue had taken, when something bumped rudely into the back of my legs.

I turned to see the henna-haired lady with the walker, and she had a mean look on her face. She looked like an ancient version of Lucille Ball who'd just heard her show was canceled.

"Can I help you?" I asked politely, ignoring the fact that she had run into me.

"Yes!" she snapped. "You can help me by painting the frickin' room. I'm missing the gosh-darn Game Channel!"

Only she didn't say "frickin' " or "gosh-darn," either.

I *could* have tipped her over with one finger, but remembering the Golden Rule, hurried to catch up with Mother.

A Trash 'n' Treasures Tip

Bringing along a few useful tools to a flea market can save you a lot of time and heartache. These include a notebook, tape measure, magnifying glass, tote bag for small items, plus packing material and sacks for breakables.

Mother once put a delicate figurine in her

coat pocket, thinking it to be safe, then got in the car, and sat on it. (Go ahead and smile — I did.)

CHAPTER SEVEN:
CUCKOO CLOCKED

When I awoke the next morning — roused by a wet-nosed Sushi — there was a Post-it from Mother stuck to the coffeepot (the first place I go), telling me that she would be gone for most of the day "on business." Which of course meant sticking her nose into other people's business.

That gave me an excuse to enjoy a lazy day of peace and quiet, and provided time to catch up on some important reading I'd been putting off — namely, my fashion magazines.

After feeding Sushi, then giving her a shot, followed by a dog biscuit (the promise of which made her actually *want* to get stuck), I made myself some burnt (on purpose) cinnamon toast, which I nibbled between gulps of strong hot coffee. Then I went back upstairs to bed, not to sleep — I'd had my morning coffee, remember? — but to work on perfecting laziness as an art form.

Sushi soon joined me, jumping up on the rumpled covers, wanting to play, so I set aside the latest issue of *In Style,* slipped my hand under the blanket, and pretended my arm was a stalking snake. Soosh was pretty good at sensing where my fingers-shaped-like-a-python's-mouth would strike next, and more than once I went "Ouch!" when her sharp little teeth pierced through the cover.

The downstairs phone interrupted our fun, and I went out into the hallway and stood at the top of the stairwell to listen to the message that was already coming in on the answer machine below. (If it was for Mother, I never picked up; why subject myself to her later endless interrogation over what "exactly" the caller had said? Let the tape tell her.)

But when I heard the quavering voice of Mrs. Lange, I rushed to pick up the extension by the upstairs bathroom. Instant guilt poked through the layers of Prozac and indolence — I had never followed up on Joe having been spotted at the trailer park the night of the murder.

"This is Brandy," I said.

A sigh of relief flooded the line. "Oh, thank goodness I *reached* you —"

"What is it, Mrs. Lange?"

The words tumbled out: "I'm so worried about Joe — he hasn't been home for over a week!"

That was alarming, all right, but to counteract her distress, I said calmly, "Is that really so unusual?"

"Oh, yes, and he's *completely* off his medication. But even so, he always comes back home."

"To see how you're doing," I said.

"For food and water!" The woman rushed on, "You see, I normally set out his favorite food on the kitchen counter every few days, wrapped sandwiches or maybe Lunchables and bottled water and a thermos of hot coffee, and then in the morning, they'd be gone." Her voice cracked in a sob. "But last week's food is *still there!*"

This was yet another deviation from Joe's pattern, which could spell trouble. So could a week, even with a wrapped sandwich.

I said, "He's probably camped out in Wild Cat Den." If he'd gone full-throttle survivalist, he'd be having squirrel-kabobs and the like. No need for her, or me, to panic. Right?

Right?

"Wild Cat Den's where he usually goes," she was agreeing, "but he's never gone off his medication in the winter before." A little sob escaped. "And it's *freezing* out now!"

I said gently, "I'm sure he's fine. He's trained himself to withstand all kinds of conditions. . . . Have you tried contacting the park ranger?"

"Yes, but I didn't get an answer, so I just left a message."

It was time to please Mother and displease Brian and do some Nancy Drewing. "Would you like me to go out there and see if I can find Joe?"

"Oh, *would* you?" she asked. "That would be wonderful." She paused, adding tentatively, "Otherwise, Brandy, I don't have any choice — I'll have to contact the sheriff, and that will mean filing *commitment* papers again, and —"

"Let me try to bring your son home first."

"Thank you, Brandy. You've always been a good friend to Joe. How I wish you two kids could have settled down together."

"Let me get back to you," I said, really wishing she hadn't shared that last thought with me.

In my bedroom, buried in the back of the closet, was a ski outfit that I'd only worn once, probably because it was a neon lime green. I'd purchased it since it seemed only fair warning, letting others see an out-of-control Brandy-on-skis coming at them. I climbed into the insulated pants and jacket, then sat on the edge of the bed to lace up my waterproof hiking boots.

That's when Sushi went ballistic, dancing and yapping in front of me like a puppet operated by a puppeteer having a seizure. You see, I only put on those boots when I take her out to Wild Cat Den. What tells the blind pooch I'm putting on those particular shoes — the smell of the rubber? The sound of the laces?

"No, girl, you can't go," I said, adding ridiculously, "This is business." Surely she would understand.

Well, for sure she understood the word "no," and in a flash of brown and white fur, the dog disappeared into my closet, and in moments was backing out, dragging the Stuart Weitzman black loafer by her sharp little teeth, and — with a great deal of effort, which I could only grudgingly admire — placed the shoe right front of me, then flopped on top of it, her jaws opened, ready to munch.

I stood, hands on hips, and looked down, and growled at her.

She growled back.

"Soosh, that's *blackmail!*"

With a further little growl, she dug her fangs into the expensive soft leather.

184

"All right!" I hollered. She did not make empty threats. "All right! I'll take you."

Sushi released the loafer.

I waggled a finger as if she could see it. "But it won't be as much fun as in the summertime," I warned her. "And you'll have to wear that *coat* you hate, to keep warm."

I left Soosh to think that over.

In the kitchen I packed some leftover meat loaf, stale potato chips, and rebottled faucet water in a small backpack, in case I found a malnourished Joe. We didn't keep Lunchables around.

Sushi was waiting by the coat closet, apparently agreeable to my terms, and I got out the small red doggie jacket that had five legs because I had knitted it while watching a cable showing of the original *Night of the Living Dead,* and perhaps wasn't paying attention to what I was doing.

But Sushi couldn't see my five-legged mistake, or else interpreted the extra opening as if intended for her tail, and I received nary a yip nor a yap as I stuffed her into the coat. Then, not wanting Soosh to get too overheated, I quickly wrote Mother a note telling her where we were going (didn't want Mother getting overheated, either), and left it on the downstairs toilet seat lid, the first place *she'd* go when home from her day of snooping.

Soon Sushi and I were tooling along the River Road, me enjoying the snowy, woodsy landscape, and Soosh enjoying the warmth of the sun bathing her through the windshield. I had one of those "Cocktail Christmas" CDs going in the dash player, with the likes of Frank Sinatra and Dean Martin and Lena Horne doing seasonal standards in a swinging way. They served to help lighten my mood, since I was both a little afraid and somewhat guilty about Joe's potential status in the wilds of Wild Cat Den.

After about fifteen miles, a well-worn sign pointing to the state park appeared, and I turned onto a blacktop road. A few more miles later, I glided by the old Pine Creek Grist Mill, situated on the banks of a now-frozen stream, the mill's giant wooden wheel motionless for the season.

Then a small log cabin home came into view. This was where Park Ranger Edwina Forester lived. That's right — Forester. Deal with it.

No? Then let's discuss for a few moments the correlation of a person's name and his or her personality and/or destiny. I knew this guy in high school whose last name was Rushing, and honestly, he was always in a big hurry to go nowhere in particular. Then there was this girl at community college I was friends with for a while, but had to drop, because she drove me bananas taking so long to make up her mind about even the simplest of things. Her last name? Mull. So, is it just a coincidence that Edwina Forester became a park ranger? I think not. If you don't believe me, check with that old dickens Charles.

"Eddie" to her friends (Miss Forester or Miss Park Ranger to me) was fortyish and wirily muscular, a former Marine and one-time truck driver, who was tough but fair with the park-going public, unless she caught someone with alcohol, at which time she went all Marine Corps on their behind. (I still regretted bringing that the bottle of champagne along on that one picnic.)

Since I didn't see the ranger's Range Rover (beginning to see a pattern here?), I thought I'd leave the woman a note on her door, explaining that I was poking around the park (usually fairly unpopulated this time of year) looking for Joe. Hastily, I scribbled my message on a Dunkin' Donuts napkin with an eyeliner pencil, because I didn't have a real writing implement.

Sushi — who had jumped out of the car as soon as I'd opened my door and followed me up the stone-lined walk — also left the park ranger a little something on her front stoop: a tiny brown turdlet, which I kicked snow over because I didn't have another napkin to pick it up with.

Back in the car, I asked, "Did you *have* to do that?"

Sushi, seated in profile next to me on the passenger side, had her lower jaw set in a pout.

"Just because she wasn't there to give you a bone," I gently scolded, "doesn't mean you have to try to get even."

The jaw jutted out further giving her a comical, snaggle-toothed look, and I had to laugh. She shot me a white-eyed look that let me know in no uncertain terms that her not getting a bone was no laughing matter.

Soon we were driving through the park's main entrance, its steel gate halfheartedly open, inviting in only the brave and the idiotic on this icy, cold day. At a fork in the road, I slowed the car, contemplating my options: The road to the right led to the top of the park, while the one to the left went to the lower level. Since Joe, I felt sure, would most likely be holed up in one of the limestone caves located in between the two levels, and accessible only on foot, my options were to slip-slide down to him, or climb-claw up. I decided the latter would be easier on both Soosh and me.

The lower level of the park was deserted, the crusted snow showing only a few tire tracks from recent hardy (or foolhardy) visitors. I eased my Buick up to one of the wooden railroad ties that designated a parking spot.

Then, with my knapsack of food slung over one shoulder, and Sushi tucked inside my zipped-up ski jacket (her head protruding like a baby alien that had burst from my chest), I stood for a moment at the base of the high bluff, contemplating my route of ascent.

There were three paths from which to choose: "difficult," a steep, rocky climb upward; "not as difficult," a combination of steep and gradual; and "just give up, already," a meandering trail akin to a wheelchair ramp.

Choosing the mid-level trek, I started up the snowy trail, but it wasn't long before I was huffing and puffing, my breath coming like train-stack smoke. Upon reaching "Fat Man's Squeeze," a narrow fissure in the bluff wall that allowed an upward shortcut for the slender (that I hadn't been able to use since the seventh grade), I flopped on a wooden bench to give my burning thigh muscles a rest.

After a few minutes, Sushi yapped that she was hot and wanted out of my jacket, and I had to agree, the sun now high in the sky, its rays slanting down like well-aimed arrows through the bare trees, hitting us with a warmth that was surprising considering how my breath still showed.

I put Soosh down on the path, which had only a dusting of snow, and she was immediately familiar with where she was, trotting on ahead on the trail we had so often taken during warmer months. I stood, then quickly caught up to her.

Since we were nearing the flattened-out portion of the bluff where the caves were located — and where I hoped to find Joe — I thought it prudent to announce my presence, because there's nothing quite so heartwarming as surprising a jumpy ex-serviceman — and an unstable one at that.

To let him know I was a "friendly," I began to sing a snappy version of "The Caisson Song":

Over hill, over dale
as we hit the snowy trail,
(*I took a liberty with 'dusty trail'*)
those caissons go rolling along!
(*What's a caisson, anyway?*)

Then it's hi! hi! hee!
in the field artillery
(*Who knew war could be so much fun?*)
shout out your numbers loud and clear!
For where 'ere we go
you will always know
that those caissons go rolling along!

I realized that Joe had been in the National Guard, but since I didn't know their official song — or even if there was one (I was in no position to Google it) — I segued into "The Marine Hymn," which I basically knew from old Bugs Bunny cartoons:

From the halls of Montezuma
to the shores of Tripoli,
We will fight our nation's battles
in the air, on land, and sea.

Here, I lost my way with the words ("Da da da da da da *dah* da da!") and finally trailed off, which was just as well because 1) we had reached the string of caves, and 2) Sushi had begun to sing along in a high-pitched howl that hurt my eardrums.

To get her to stop, I said, "Find Joe, girl! Find *Joe,* and we can have our lunch!"

Well, blind eyes were no obstacle for a twenty-twenty canine stomach, and she took off like a heat-seeking missile, sniffing at the mouth of this cave and that one, finally halting at an opening in the limestone cliff that I had never noticed before because it was partially hidden behind some large rocks that had fallen from the bluff above.

I joined Soosh and whispered, "Is he in there, girl?"

She yapped once. If I could play Nancy Drew, Soosh could damn well play Lassie.

Setting my food bag aside, I went over and dropped down on my knees in front of the hole, which was just large enough for a person to crawl through.

"*Joe!*" I called. "Are you in there? It's *me* — Brandy."

I thought I heard a rustling from within, and Sushi confirmed it with a growl that became a yap.

"Joe . . . *please* come out. . . . I have some *provisions. . . . ?*"

No sound at all now.

I didn't relish the idea of exploring this or any cave, especially if "Joe" turned out to be a hibernating bear, unhappy to get an early wake-up call.

But Joe *could* be inside, and possibly sick or hurt.

"Okay," I said, "If you're not coming out, I'm coming in. . . ."

Cautiously, I crawled into the darkness of the cave like Alice in Wonderland going down the rabbit hole (and we all know how well that played out — off with her head!).

And almost off with mine: I heard a swish and perceived a hard blow to the back of my head, and then I was in my own personal dark cave.

When I came to, I was propped against the wall of rock, my legs splayed out, my aching head turned toward a flickering light.

A candle in a glass jar came gradually into focus, and my eyes worked well enough to read "Home for the Holidays," written across a picture of a cheery, fireside hearth.

Slowly, painfully, I straightened my neck, and took in my surroundings as best I could. The cave was small, as caves go, about half the size of my bedroom, its low jagged ceiling preventing me from standing (the cave, not my bedroom). By the shimmer of candlelight, I could make out army gear stashed everywhere: canteens and ration kits, goggles and binoculars, ropes and netting, along with a good deal of camping supplies. Clearly, Joe was dug in here for the long winter haul.

But what made the hairs stand up on the back of my *really* sore (and now tingling) neck were the military weapons piled in one corner: assault rifles, bayonets, guns, and knives . . . plus something on a tripod that looked really nasty.

Joe said, "M-249 SAW, Squad Automatic Weapon."

Clad military-style, he was on his haunches, animal-like, munching at my bag of stale potato chips, his long hair greasy and tangled, features obliterated by camouflage paint, except for his eyes.

His wild, unstable eyes.

Doing my best to mask my fear, I snapped crossly, "What didja hit me for? I'm a *friendly.*"

Joe put down the chips and crawled over like a spider, and settled down before a very frightened Little Miss Tuffet.

"Who *sent* you?" he asked, eyes narrowing suspiciously, the candlelight throwing eerie shadows on his face.

Joe — unmedicated Joe — had never frightened me before. I'd sometimes found him unsettlingly odd, sure, but then I had never before seen him this bad. And I had not taken at all seriously the notion that Joe might have killed Mr. Yaeger over that Tarzan book. My assumption had always been that there was an innocent reason for his presence at Happy Trails Trailer Park. Now

I wasn't so sure.

I chose my words carefully.

"No one sent me, Joe," I said evenly. "I came here on my own scouting mission."

He nodded, accepting that.

"Where's Sushi?" I asked.

"The little dog?" He jerked his head toward the entrance of the cave. "Out there — with Charlie. But she'll never make it back through enemy lines."

So Sushi had gotten away, and would probably return to the car and take shelter beneath it, her coat-of-five-legs to keep her warm until someone came.

I said, "Maybe she'll bring back help," and immediately regretted it, because Joe turned agitated.

"We don't need backup!" he barked. "Got everything right here!"

This "we" business at least meant I had moved from the enemy column over to fellow combatant. Now all I needed was to get the hell out of here, on the double. . . .

I said with urgency, "Joe, I have to get to a medic. I think I have a concussion."

But my friend had lost interest in me, crawling back to the bag of chips.

I had lapsed into silence, wondering what to do, when a shout came from outside the cave.

"Joe!"

Someone was using a bullhorn. I couldn't tell who, but we had been found! Only, what if Joe blamed me for leading these unfriendlies to his hidey-hole?

"Joe!" the bullhorn called again.

I looked anxiously at my cave mate for his response, which was to scrounge in a duffel bag, then scurry over to my side, where he pressed something into my hand.

"What's this?" I frowned at the capsule in my palm.

"Cyanide. If we get stormed, bite down on it."

"What?"

"If you don't, Brandy, I'll have to shoot you in the head. Can't let Charlie take you alive." Joe was saying this as calmly as if reading me the current weather report. Then he got glinty-eyed. "Do you have any *idea* what they'd do to you? Makes Gitmo look like a tea party."

Alice in Wonderland again, only she got the Mad Hatter and I got Off His Rocker Rambo.

Well, I least I was still a valued friendly, valued so much that he would kill me to save me.

I watched in horror as he scrambled back across the cave's floor to the weapons stash, where he snatched up one of the military guns.

"Corporal Lange!" the bullhorn blared. *"This is Marine Sergeant Forester!"*

The Marines had landed! Or, anyway, the park ranger lady. . . .

"I order you to come out of that cave, soldier, or you'll be reported AWOL!"

Joe froze in a half-crouch, the gun pointed at the cave's entrance.

Terrified that Joe might fire at the park ranger — or my head — I said, "She *does* outrank you, Joe. Do you *really* want to risk a court-martial?"

Seconds dragged by like minutes; then Joe released his tight grip on the gun and set it down.

"There's a civilian in here!" he yelled. "Brandy Borne."

"Is she hurt?"

Joe looked my way, and for the first time had concern in his eyes. "Brandy . . . ?"

I hollered, "I'm okay!"

The bullhorn crackled, *"Send her out."*

Joe gave me a crisp nod, his eyes nominally more normal now in that green-and-brown-and-black face.

I crawled toward the cave's mouth, wondering if the last sound I'd ever hear would be a gunshot reverberating in that tiny cave as Joe shot me from behind.

But moments later, I was outside the cave's modest entrance, and rising slowly to my feet, which were as wobbly as a newborn calf's. I squinted, protecting my face with a hand, my eyes adjusting to the light. The sun was setting on Joe Lange's mission.

Edwina Forester, wearing an olive-green Marine service coat instead of her brown park ranger jacket, gestured with the bullhorn for me get out of harm's way, or anyway hers, and I stumbled down the path toward a waiting Sheriff Rudder, who was holding Sushi.

Soosh, who soon smelled me, squirmed out of the sheriff's grasp and into mine, licking happy tears from my face.

Edwina, now dispensing with the bullhorn, called, "Joe! Fall in! On the double!"

After a few more long seconds, Joe's head protruded from the cave like a turtle from its shell; then the rest of him emerged. Finally, he got to his feet, straightened his back, and gave his superior officer a smart salute.

"At ease," Edwina barked.

Joe's body relaxed.

"I'm relieving you of duty, Corporal, as of now. You've done an A-number-one job of patrolling this park, and deserve ninety-six for a little R 'n' R."

"Yes, sir!"

"You *will* go with Sheriff Rudder for debriefing. And you *will* have to pass a complete physical before returning to duty. Is that understood?"

"Yes, sir!"

"All right, soldier. Dismissed!"

I watched in amazement as the sheriff — with a simple, "Come on, son" — led a seemingly docile Joe down the path.

Edwina stood beside me and settled a gentle hand on my shoulder. "Are you all right, Ms. Borne?"

"My head really hurts. He slugged me from behind and knocked me out."

She lifted my hair for a look. "That's a nasty bump. Can you make it to the bottom, or should I call for paramedics and a gurney?"

"No, I think I could make it . . . but could you carry Sushi? I still feel kinda dizzy. . . ."

I handed the pooch over, then took one step, and collapsed in the snow.

I woke up in the ER with an IV in my arm. Brian, in uniform, was seated next to me on the stainless-steel stool reserved for the doctor, who was nowhere in sight.

I mumbled, "What . . . what happened. . . . ?"

Brian leaned in and smiled reassuringly. "You just fainted. They'll be giving you a CT scan in a minute. . . ."

I took a deep breath, which hurt my head. "Mother . . . ?"

"Your sister is trying to find her."

Good luck to her.

"What am I going to do with you?" Brian asked, quietly exasperated. "Why didn't you have me go with you to find Joe? You could've been killed."

I closed my eyes. "Listen, there's more I should have told you. Joe was at that trailer park the night —"

"Mr. Yeager was killed," he finished. "We know. That's why I alerted Ranger Forester and Sheriff Rudder to keep an eye on Wild Cat Den. Everybody knows it's Joe's favorite haunt."

"So Chaz isn't your only suspect?"

Brian sighed. "I suppose you should know that Yeager's missing Tarzan book turned up in that cave."

"Joe *did* have it? Where?"

"In his duffel bag."

Along with that cyanide capsule.

So had Joe poisoned Mr. Yeager for the purloined loincloth saga, after which he went off the deep end? If so, *I* had set the whole thing in motion! I was worse than Mother. . . .

A white-coated female doctor appeared and announced, "Time for your X-ray, Ms. Borne," and two male attendants in green scrubs took either end of my gurney and began rolling it out into the hallway.

Brian tagged along beside me.

I looked up at him. "Joe tried to make me take a pill. . . ."

Brian frowned down. "What was it?"

"I don't know. He told me it was cyanide."

Then I was going through the double doors of the X-ray room, leaving a stunned Brian behind.

A Trash 'n' Treasures Tip

Bring only cash to flea markets. While many antiques stores and malls will accept checks and charge cards, flea market vendors are a wary bunch, and some don't take kindly to large-denomination bills. Or to the IRS, for that matter.

Chapter Eight: Sentimental Jury

Mother has always insisted on having her very own chapter, but lately she's been hounding me for another. Honestly, I didn't think you could take it . . . so for now, one chapter is all she gets. (The usual disclaimers apply.)

Brandy has been pushing my chapter later and later in these books, which I hardly think is fair. After all, it's very poor construction to keep the heroine off center stage until Act Three! Additionally, how am I expected to share everything that's on my mind in a few paltry pages? (Brandy has given me a strict seven-thousand-word limit.) Furthermore, I *am* privy to information to which my daughter has no access, so I think it's only reasonable for me to write one chapter early on, and then another one later. (If you agree with my thinking, gentle reader, please contact the publisher and request more of Vivian Borne. And I do apologize for dragging you into this.)

Of late I have been extremely concerned about Brandy; the poor child seems to be careening out of control. I had hoped that her recent detente with Roger, her ex-husband, and her improved relationship with Jake, her son, would rescue Brandy from her doldrums, but in fact the girl seems more depressed than ever.

Consequently, I have been checking her plastic pill box on the kitchen counter, making sure she has been taking her anti-depressant medication — surprisingly, she has been — so I can only assume the dosage should be increased, as mine has been on rare occasions. (Once, when our pill boxes were the same color, we got them mixed up, and that Prozac of hers put me to sleep for twelve hours; when I awoke I found Brandy in the backyard in her bathing suit, chasing a squirrel that I'm not convinced was really there.) But I digress.

After visiting Brandy in the hospital and determining that her noggin would soon be more or less in working order, I returned home to take care of sweet little Sushi, after which I headed to bed for a good night's sleep, knowing the next day would be a very busy one indeed.

When I questioned Brandy about the events at Wild Cat Den, she was rather evasive (not unusual), saying only that she'd apparently startled Joe in his cave, which is why he'd conked her. But she *did* let slip one juicy piece of info: The missing Tarzan book had been found among Joe's things. Which had pushed our little British bird from the top slot on the suspect list, making Joe number one with a bullet.

Well, I could no more believe Joe killed Walter than Chaz had! So once again, Vivian Borne had to rise to the occasion, uncover the truth, and free the unjustly accused.

The following morning, after a hardy breakfast of pancakes and sausage (a girl has to keep up her strength, you know), I let Sushi outdoors one last time, as that dog has to urinate more often than *moi.* Then I climbed into my warm raccoon coat, tied my favorite blue woolen scarf over my head, and slipped on Brandy's pair of comfortable, ever-so-toasty brown UGGS (she wouldn't be wearing them today, now would she?).

The weather was crisp and clear, sun shining bright as a new penny, if a penny were orange and not copper. Brandy's boots crunched through a thin layer of freshly fallen snow, as I hurried along the sidewalk to catch the traveling trolley a few blocks away, due at any moment.

The old reconverted-to-gas trolley car (I wonder if I'll be around long enough to see it converted back to electric?) was free of charge to anyone wanting to go downtown (my usual destination), but I could sometimes sweet-talk the driver into dropping me elsewhere, if it weren't too far off the beaten path.

Roxanne Randolph was the first person to drive the trolley, but she quit suddenly after going home early one afternoon to nurse a migraine only to find her husband in the steamy clutches of a young neighbor who, in fact, *was* a nurse. Hubby tried telling Roxanne that the lady was just giving him mouth-to-mouth resuscitation (hubby had heart problems) (obviously), but Roxie didn't buy it. Then Roxie did some amateur nursing herself, cleaning hubby out like a colonic, and she's now living in Arizona, very happily I hear.

Maynard Kirby went after the trolley job next because he had to go back to work after his wife gambled away all his retirement money from his long tenure at the fish hatchery. But then he, too, quit suddenly, after his wife spawned big bucks in the state lottery. Thank God for her addiction!

Currently, a young black woman named Shawntea Monroe drove the trolley car. I met her in Chicago the previous summer when four of us Red-Hatted League gals drove into the Windy City for a Cubs game and lost our bearings (I was navigating, possibly a mistake pre-cataract surgery) and we ladies found ourselves with a flat tire somewhere called Cabrini-Green.

Well, Shawntea — who had just disembarked a gas-belching bus — took pity on us out-of-water fishies, and got her brother, Trayvon (member of a young men's club called Gangsta Disciples), to change our tire and get us girls headed off in the right direction.

But before we drove away, I gave Shawntea my phone number and let her know that should she ever want to get a fresh start in new surroundings, I'd send her a one-way bus ticket to Serenity with a promise of work, feeling fairly certain I could help her find some. Shawntea did call, a few months later, about the same time the trolley job opened up, and that's what we call Serenity serendipity.

As I climbed aboard the trolley, Shawntea — wearing a warm purple parka, her lovely black hair cascading in tight curls — gave me her winning white smile. "Hello, Miz Borne. How's it shakin'?"

"Shaking quite nicely, Shawntea," I said, and slid into the seat directly behind her. At the moment, the trolley was toting only a few passengers, this being an off-time for travel, what with people already at work and the downtown shops not quite open.

"And how are Kwamie and Zeffross?" I asked. To my surprise, she had arrived in town with two young boys in tow.

"Oh, Miz Borne, they jus' love their new school," Shawntea said, pulling the trolley away from the curb.

"And how are *your* night classes going?"

"One more semester, and I get my GED."

"Wonderful! And what then?"

She hesitated. "Kinda thinkin' about community college."

"Well, you're certain to get a scholarship."

She glanced back. "You really think so?"

"I can practically guarantee it." I knew all of the college foundation board members, several of whom had the kind of skeletons in their closets that no one likes to hear come rattling out.

"That would be *dope,* Miz Borne," she said.

"Dope, dear?"

"Cool. Great. Awesome."

"Stick with those terms, Shawntea. 'Dope' has different connotations in these parts."

"Oh. Yes. Well, sure."

"It implies stupidity, dear."

"It sure does."

We rumbled along Elm Street, a straight shot downtown, passing by lovely old homes, most sporting festive green wreaths on their doors, trees lavish in front windows, yards arrayed with Nativity scenes or Santa with his sleigh and reindeer.

As we turned right on Main, Shawntea asked, "Where ya want to be dropped, Miz Borne?"

"The courthouse will be just fine, dear." The trolley's first downtown stop.

Bidding Shawntea adieu, I disembarked the trolley, then hoofed it over to the county jail, nicely positioned across from the courthouse, making hauling criminals into court most convenient — hardly any inmates ever escaped just crossing the street.

I had worked tirelessly for the new county jail — a two-story, red-brick, state-of-the-art, fenceless facility that looked more like an administrative building than a detention center. I'd done this in part because I felt that even convicts deserved better living conditions than the old, crumbling jail. But, also, I had once ended up in those squalid former quarters and, frankly, it was equally appalling for non-convicts like me.

The new jail's lobby might have been an airport gate waiting area, with its rows of seating back-to-back, vending machines, small lockers for storing personal items, and walk-through security scanner.

I strolled over to the young man (nonuniformed) who acted as a reception- ist, and spoke through the tiny microphone in the glass. "Vivian Borne would like a word with Sheriff Rudder."

The man looked up at me, narrowing his already narrow eyes. "He's awfully busy, ma'am. . . ."

"Oh, he'll see me," I said. "We're old friends."

And I turned abruptly to take a seat in the boarding area, hoping the wait wouldn't be as long as at O'Hare.

A good half hour crawled by before the sheriff buzzed himself through the steel door into the reception room. As he ap- proached, I stood and, not wanting to waste any more of my precious time, came right to the point.

"I need to see Joe Lange," I told him. "I assume you've had time enough to get him through processing."

Sheriff Rudder, a tall, confident man who

reminded me of Randolph Scott (circa *Ride the High Country*) (except that his eyes were a trifle crossed), furrowed the brow of his rugged face. "I don't think a visit with Joe's possible right now, Vivian. Maybe in a few days. What's this about?"

"I'm sure poor Joe would like to hear that Brandy is unhurt and will be out of the hospital tomorrow. And by the way . . . thank you for your part in rescuing my daughter. She's very precious to me."

The sheriff considered my request momentarily, then nodded. "Joe *has* been asking about Brandy, but he's in a fairly upset state. I'd prefer to pass along the information myself."

I stood my ground. "Considering Joe's present mental condition — that is to say, extreme paranoia — I'm afraid he would only believe the good news about Brandy if it came from the horse's mouth. *I* am that horse."

Rudder chuckled and said, "Which end, Vivian?"

"What did you say, Sheriff?"

"Uh . . . to what end, Vivian?"

"Well . . . if Joe is at all anxious, my visit might calm him down. You may not realize this, but I have, in my time, suffered minor mental problems myself."

"Really? Well. Who'd have thought it."

"There are mental health interest groups who would *not* take kindly to —"

The sheriff held up a palm. "All right, Vivian . . . but only for a few minutes."

Shortly thereafter, another steel door at the back of the waiting area opened, and a pretty, ponytailed female deputy came out, greeted me perfunctorily, took my fur coat, scarf, and purse, put them in one of the lockers, and handed me the small key. I was then ordered to step through the metal detector.

"That's not a good idea," I said to her.

"It's required."

Well, wouldn't you just know that the extensive bridgework in my mouth set the thing to buzzing, which took another few minutes getting straightened out. Finally, the deputy was ushering me through to the inner jail, using a security card.

We passed through two more locked doors before arriving in an area consisting of three small visitor's stations, like those claustrophobic closets the bank teller insists on putting me into when I want to go over my will.

The deputy deposited me on a chair facing the glass window separating me from the prisoner's side (and it from me); then she retreated to stand outside my cubicle, granting some privacy.

Joe, wearing an orange jumpsuit, was escorted to his chair on the other side of the glass by a beefy, bucket-headed male deputy. This deputy did not afford Joe any breathing space, positioning himself directly behind the young man.

Joe looked pale, and seemed withdrawn, even subdued; but his drugged eyes — indicating he was already back on his medication — showed a flash of life when he saw it was me.

We both reached for our phones.

He spoke first. "Is Brandy okay?"

"Yes, Joe — fit as a fiddle. Home tomorrow."

He began to cry, his shoulders rising and falling. "Mrs. Borne, will . . . will Brandy ever for . . . for*give* me?"

"Of course, dear," I said gently. "Just like she always forgives me. She understands you and I are a little bit . . ."

"Different?"

"I was going to say 'crazy,' but that's a nice way of putting it. Now dry your tears."

Joe wiped his eyes with a sleeve of his orange jumpsuit.

With some urgency, sitting so close my forehead almost touched the glass, I said, "Joe, I only have a precious few minutes. . . ."

He nodded. His eyes were hazy, but at least they met my gaze unflinchingly.

"I want you to tell me the truth, Joe. Did you poison Walter Yeager?"

The eyes unclouded. "*No,* Mrs. Borne! I didn't! I swear it on my oath as a soldier."

"But you *did* take that book, didn't you, dear?"

He swallowed thickly, then his head dropped . . . and he nodded. "Yes. I was just going to talk to the old gent, make him an offer — I have some money saved up I use for collectibles. I buy and sell on eBay, you know. But then I *saw* it, just lying on the table. . . ."

"What about Mr. Yaeger?"

Joe looked up again. "The old man was dead when I got there. I swear it!" Wildness came to the eyes. "As God is my witness, Mrs. Borne, I even tried to save him. I called for help, but, but, but . . ."

Joe bolted to his feet, the phone receiver dropping from his hand, swinging by its cord like a hung man. (Or is it "hanged"? I'm never quite sure. . . .)

"*Medic!*" he cried, his eyes crazed, his voice muffled by the glass. "Man down! Bring in Medevac! Cue the damn chopper!"

The beefy deputy grabbed Joe, quickly

cuffing the young man's hands and then hauling the squirmy prisoner from the cubicle.

My ponytailed deputy came in and glared at me. "I thought you were going to *calm* him!"

I stood and spread my hands. "How was *I* to know Joe would go jungle-happy? One can never predict how an unbalanced individual might behave. Might I suggest that his medication be increased?"

The deputy squinched her face, her attractive features suddenly becoming most unattractive. "Oh, *thank* you. I'll be sure to pass your recommendation along to the doctor."

"Please do. And, dear? You'll develop the most unsightly wrinkles if you insist on scowling."

She marched me ever so quickly back through the locked doors and, after I gathered all of my things from the locker, escorted me to the front door, watching to make sure I'd left. At least she was efficient.

My next stop was the Public Safety Building, conveniently located next door to the jail, where I announced through another microphone-embedded-in-glass that I wished to see Chief Cassato.

The unfamiliar female dispatcher (a Hispanic child, with short brown hair and glasses) turned away from her bank of monitors to use a phone. Then, after a muffled conversation to which I wasn't privy, she politely told me that the chief was out of the office today.

I made a mental note of the dispatcher's name tag on her crisp blue shirt; she was someone whose friendship would need to be cultivated. But first the woman had to be properly trained on how to cultivate *Vivian Borne's* friendship. . . .

I said sweetly, "The chief's car is in the parking lot, so you must be mistaken, my dear . . . would you please check again? If he's in a meeting, please let him know I am more than happy to wait *all day.*"

And, without giving the young woman a chance to reply, I turned and trod over to the small waiting area of mismatched plastic chairs, settling in next to a rubber-tree plant in dire need of some TLC. To pass the time, I retrieved a pair of small scissors from my handbag and began snipping off dead leaves.

I didn't expect much of a wait, however. Chief Cassato was no fool. You see, *I* knew that *he* knew I would linger here all day to see him . . . and *he* knew that *I* knew that *he* knew this. Clear?

So it was only a few minutes before the

heavy door leading into the inner workings of the Serenity PD opened and the chief strode out.

A big barrel-chested man and the bearer of a rumpled face that some women might find attractive, the chief wore a well-starched white long-sleeved shirt, navy tie, gray pressed slacks, and black belt with silver badge attached.

He planted himself in front of my chair, hands on hips, looked down at me with half-lidded eyes. "Well, Vivian?"

The chief was not known for his loquaciousness.

I took a moment to carefully store my scissors back in my purse, having once stabbed my hand reaching in for something else — an ounce of prevention is worth a pound of cure.

I looked up and said, "Your office?"

I could be just as unloquacious as the next fellow.

His sigh ruffled the rubber tree's leaves. But he gave up a bare nod, then preceded to turn abruptly on his Florsheims, and I had to make tracks to keep up as we went through the security door, and down the long, tan-tiled corridor to the last office on the left.

What I found most annoying about Chief

216

Anthony (middle initial unknown) Cassato was the way he so fiercely protected his privacy, like a bulldog with a ham bone. I knew practically *nothing* about the man since his sudden arrival here three years ago to head up the Serenity PD. And all that my spies could glean was that he came from somewhere in the East. Whoopee.

But there were plenty of rumors floating around about the chief. Some of the better stories I'd started myself, just to ferret out the truth (such as the chief having been put into Witness Protection because he'd ratted on the New York mob), but so far that tactic hadn't worked.

Similarly disappointing was the chief's office itself, which gave little clue as to the man's past or present: no personal photographs of family or friends, no mementos, not even any awards he had been given while serving on the force, merely a single framed duck print on the wall to the right of his desk to hint at a hobby. Of course, the picture might well have been left behind by the former chief upon retirement.

Tony Cassato gestured impatiently for me to take the padded chair in front of his desk, and was about to go behind it when Officer Munson stuck his head in the doorway.

Using an uncalled-for sharpness of tone,

the chief said to me, "One moment," then went out into the hall, where he and Munson engaged in what sounded like a serious conversation. Damn! If I'd only scheduled my semiannual earwax cleaning, I might have been able to eavesdrop.

In a flash, I was out of my chair and onto Plan B: poking through his desk drawers before you could say, "Search and seizure."

Spotting an official-looking letter postmarked from Trenton, New Jersey, I was about to pocket it when my wax-addled ears *did* perceive the men's conversation winding down.

I didn't have quite enough time to get back to my seat, so I pretended to be studying the duck print on the wall, asking, as the chief entered, "This wouldn't be an original John James Audubon, by any chance?"

Tony, eyeing me suspiciously, said sharply, "No. It wouldn't. Can we get to the point of your visit?"

I returned to my chair, and Tony settled his bulk into his.

I began, "I've just paid a visit to Joe Lange over at the county jail."

The chief showed no reaction, not even a raised eyebrow. His hands were on his desk. Or rather his fists were.

I continued, "Joe said that when he arrived at that trailer, Walter Yeager was already dead . . ." I played my best cards. ". . . and I happen to *believe* him!"

But again, no reaction.

"Joe *did* admit to taking the book," I continued.

The chief remained stony-faced.

"Which means Yeager's killer is still out there!"

The chief sighed. Then, finally, he spoke: "Is there anything else?"

I frowned. "Well . . . no."

"You know the way out."

I stood, unable to conceal my irritation. "I deserve better consideration than this, and a little common courtesy! I'm an interested, civic-minded public citizen who simply does not want to see the wrong person to go to prison!"

"Good-bye, Mrs. Borne."

I harrumphed, and was almost out of his office when Tony said softly "Vivian?"

I turned. The chief's stony expression had changed, his jaw not so firm, his eyes subtly softened.

"How's Brandy doing?"

I smiled inwardly. I'd always suspected that the town's top cop was sweet on my little Brandy, even if she'd never really noticed. And to think of all of the juicy, confidential information I might be privy to if *he* ever became my son-in-law. . . .

"Why, Brandy's doing fine," I said. "Merely a mild concussion. She'll be home tomorrow — stop by, if you like. I'm sure she'd enjoy seeing you."

"That was *damn* foolish of her, going out looking for Joe alone," he blustered, frowning. "Why didn't she call *us* first? And why the hell didn't *you* stop her? Do you want to get your daughter *killed* some day?"

Wasn't that sweet! I just *knew* the chief had a yen for Brandy. . . .

"Really." I chortled. "I'm surprised you'd even ask that! Since when could *I* ever control that girl?" (And, if we must be frank, vice versa.)

He surrendered a short, dry laugh. "Yeah, you have a point."

"Well . . ." I smiled sweet as punch. "I don't want to take up *any* more of your valuable time, Chief." I waggled a finger at him. "After all, you have a murderer to catch."

And so did I.

My next stop was Hunter's Hardware on Main Street. To get there, however, I had to walk past a large, hideous cement parking lot that had replaced the once-stately brick

YWCA, *and* a beautiful deco-style movie theater, *plus* the soda-fountain shop where I used to sip Green Rivers through a straw until my girlish face turned green. The willful destruction by the city of those three historical buildings still makes my blood boil! I tried to stop the carnage, and that's how I wound up in the old county jail. (Sorry, no details this time — I have a word-count limit to maintain!)

Main Street was bustling with bundled-up holiday shoppers, storefront windows displaying scenes of a Victorian-era Christmas. Hunter's was no exception, having a festive display of red-bow bedecked tools of days gone by. I stomped the snow from Brandy's boots, pushed open the ancient front door, and entered, a small bell tinkling my arrival.

Hunter's was a uniquely Midwestern aberration: The front of the elongated store — which hadn't been remodeled since I was in petticoats, and still retained its tin ceiling and hardwood floor — sold everything one might expect of a modern hardware business. The rear, however, was given over to a small bar area that offered hard liquor to hard workers who stopped in for supplies. (No one ever seemed to question the danger of farmers imbibing, and then going out into the world, chainsaws at the ready.)

221

Junior, a paunchy, rheumy-eyed, mottled-nosed man in his late sixties, was the proprietor, acting as both sales clerk and bartender. Today, however, the store was busier than usual, with customers buying that special tool for that special man (or woman — one doesn't necessary think of tools and men exclusively) (that may have come out wrong), and Junior had roped his wife, Mary — a squat lady a few years younger than him — into running the front while he more or less loafed in back.

I could tell at a glance that Mary was none too merry, spending all day selling hardware, so I put on my cheeriest Christmas smile, and steadied my resolve because, honestly, that lady was one nonstop complainer — how could one woman jabber on so endlessly about nothing? I sometimes thought she'd been vaccinated with a phonograph needle.

I approached Mary and asked pleasantly, "And how is the new leg?"

Mrs. Junior had worn a prosthesis ever since she lost a limb in a freak accident visiting the *Jaws* attraction at Universal theme park in Florida, once upon a time.

"Terrible," the woman said, screwing her face up like an old catcher's mitt left out in the rain. "I can't get used to the newfangled thing! Wish I'd hung on to my old leg. I don't know why Junior thought I needed a new one."

I did. So she could help out more at the store.

I decided to say something positive. "Heather Mills adapted quite well."

"Who?"

"The former Mrs. Paul McCartney, dear. She even took on ballroom dancing."

"Let her try it on *this* leg," Mary grumped.

"We should all walk a mile in each other's shoes, dear. Or shoe, as the case may be. Is Junior around?"

"In back," the woman said sourly, "where else?"

I made my escape.

I found Junior polishing glass tumblers behind the scarred mahogany bar, and when he spotted me, I got the usual bucktoothed grin. "Well, Vivian . . . what brings you in out of the cold?"

I slid up on one of the torn-leather stools. "A hot toddy," I announced. "But hold the toddy."

Alcohol did not mix well with my medication, I had learned.

The bar was quiet at this hour, the only customers being myself and perennial barfly Henry, who sat two stools down, caressing a half-glass of whiskey.

In his mid-fifties, slender, with silver hair, a beak nose, and his original set of teeth, Henry had once been a prominent surgeon before losing his license after performing a gall-bladder operation instead of the intended appendectomy.

(I have *tried,* more than once, to help the poor man overcome his alcohol dependency — always to disastrous effects, which I won't detail because of my word-count constraints. My most recent attempt, however, involved enrolling Henry in a twelve-step program, only to have Henry, at the final meeting, in order to celebrate his cure, secretly spike the punch bowl and send everyone in the group back to at least step two.)

Henry looked sideways and slurred, " 'Ows Viv?"

I responded, "Filled with the Christmas spirit, Henry." As opposed to filled with Christmas spirits.

Junior placed a steaming Shirley Temple in front of me and said, "Heard Brandy was in the hospital."

I waited for him to say more — to learn what he'd heard through his own bartender's grapevine — but his eyes remained vacant, his jaw slack.

Unfortunately, Junior had been born with neither nose nor mouth for gossip, a pity considering the business he was in. That made his only function in *my* world being someone I could use to disseminate information — or disinformation — as I saw fit.

Henry, however, should never be counted out; seated quietly, well in his cups, he took in everything anyone around him might say, the way a bar sponge absorbs a spill. The problem therein lay in how all that information sometimes got squeezed out of Henry . . . which is to say, a mixed-up mess.

"Well, if you *must* hear the details about Brandy. . . ." I said, waiting for enthusiastic cries of encouragement to erupt from Junior and Henry, but all I received were a nod from the former and a stare from the latter.

No matter.

A professional actor learns to play to even an unresponsive crowd; but what I *won't* tolerate are walkouts. You'd best be having a coronary when leaving the theater while Vivian Borne is performing! Because *I* know who you are, and I'll break character and walk downstage and call, "Good-bye, Mrs. So-and-so! Sorry you're leaving us so soon!"

Sometimes the fourth wall simply demands to be broken.

But I'm veering off point again. Word

count, precious word count.

Finally, Junior said, "Well, Vivian . . . spill." The man seemed to have some semblance of interest in my performance, which was all I needed to really launch into it.

Now, gentle reader, as I mentioned before, even *I* was a little unclear as to what exactly transpired in the cave between Brandy and Joe. So I took the liberty of contriving a few exciting parts of my own — Sushi biting Joe on the leg, for example — improvisation being an actor's prerogative should he/she sense that he/she might be losing the audience's attention. But I really brought down the house when I got back on script and announced that Joe had Walter's missing Tarzan book.

Junior exclaimed, "My God, that means Joe Lange killed Yeager!"

I took a sip of my neglected, now not-so-hot hot toddy. "Not necessarily," I replied. "Joe denies killing Walter . . . and I happen to *believe* him."

Henry, who'd remained silent throughout my oratory, hiccuped, then slurred, " 'S'got a se . . . crut."

Junior and I exchanged puzzled glances at this seeming non sequitur.

I said, "Yes, Henry, I'm sure Joe Lange has many a secret locked inside his poor troubled mind."

"Not Joe," Henry said. "Walt . . . Walter."

I swiveled to face him. "What kind of secret?"

Henry shook his head vigorously, as if trying to clear bats from his belfry. "Don' . . . don' know."

Sighing in disappointment, I swiveled back to my cooled-off drink. I was about to ask Junior to reheat the concoction, when Henry again spoke.

"One time? Started to tell me, but . . . didn't."

"When was this?" I asked.

"Winter '85." Henry seemed to be sobering up, or perhaps just remembering how to form complete words and semblances of sentences. "I was working ER, Walter comes in. Serious case of pneumonia. Thought he was gonna die . . . and, tell ya the truth, so did I." Henry paused, took a gulp of his whiskey, then continued: "While I was tending to him, he kept tryin' to tell me something . . . but I couldn't be swayed from my duty." Frankly, "duty" sounded a little more like "doody."

"You mean," I asked, pressing, "Walter wanted to talk to you *confidentially?* He wasn't just telling you where it hurt?"

"Maybe he was, in a way."

"What were his words *exactly?*" I pressed.

"I don't know!" So much thinking and talking had made Henry suddenly irritable. "I was busy! Tryin' to save the man's life."

"Think back, please," I said, adding sympathetically. "I know it's been a few years, but it's important . . . *try.*"

Henry frowned in thought. "He said, 'Somebody else needs to know. Can't take it to my grave.' More or less."

Junior had been quiet until now. "You ever ask Walter what he meant, later on, after he recovered?"

Henry nodded. "I did. A few months after."

"And?" I prodded.

Henry shrugged grandly and almost fell off the stool. "Denied ever sayin' such things. But claimed not to remember, either. Said he musta been delusional, 'cause of the high fever. And that was possible. So, naturally, I jus' dropped it." Henry finished his whiskey, set the glass down with a clink. "Guess we'll *never* know."

But I knew some people who might.

I turned back to Junior. "Where are the Romeos having lunch?"

He shrugged, not so grandly. "What's today?"

"Tuesday."

"They go for the meat loaf at Riverside, Tuesdays."

Why Junior could keep track of the Romeos' daily lunch schedule, and not his own anniversary, was a mystery even Vivian Borne did not care to try unraveling.

"Thanks," I said, tossing a fin on the counter. (All true detectives call five-dollar bills "fins.")

The Romeos — Retired Old Men Eating Out — were friends of long standing who generally didn't like any women coming around when they got together.

Except for one certain female: little old me. Seems these old Casanovas didn't mind *my* company, as long as I delivered some juicy tidbit of news, which I always did (even if I had to make it up), to keep my good standing with them.

While women have long worn, unfairly I would insist, the mantle of Gossip Monger, the truth is that men are often far worse, although they do have an offhand subtlety about it that females largely lack.

Entering the restaurant, which carried its riverboat theme to extremes, I quickly spotted the Romeos sequestered at a round table for six in back, and made my way toward them, skirting a fountain with a miniature paddle wheel (that on occasion had sunk).

The lunch hour was winding down, the men enjoying coffee after their fattening meal. I was glad I didn't have to watch them eat, which is never pretty, often more food going *on* their faces than making the journey inside their mouths, and the noisy clacking of plates at their table had more to do with dentures than dishes . . . but again I digress.

The Romeos were a small group today, partially due to the flu that had been going around, but mostly because the Grim Reaper had dwindled their numbers in recent years. Only present today were Vern, a retired chiropractor, who looked like the older Clark Gable if I took off my glasses; Harold, a former army captain, with Bob Hope's eyes and ski-nosed good looks when I squinted; and ex-mayor Ivan, a dead ringer for Jimmy Stewart, from a distance.

Ivan was the first to see me, and waved; Harold and Vern similarly beckoned me over. I draped my raccoon coat over the back of an empty chair, giving them my best Mae West "Hello, *boys!*"

This always got a big laugh out of them, and today was no exception.

Harold, patting the seat of the vacant chair between himself and Vern, said, "Nice to see you, Vivian. Set 'er right down. You know, we were just talking about you and

Brandy. . . ."

Frankly, I would have been shocked if we *hadn't* been the topic of conversation.

After Harold's wife died, I'd dated the former captain for a while, with an eye on matrimony, but I broke it off after a few weeks because he barked too much (you can take the man out of the army, but not the army out of the man), and Vivian Borne doesn't take orders from *anybody.*

Vern said, "We heard Brandy'll be out of the hospital tomorrow."

Vern, too, had wanted to marry me, but I threw cold water on the chiropractor's amour, which coincidentally was what the fire department also had to do, at his place of business, when the building spontaneously combusted; poor dear was a terrible pack rat. (There's only room for one pack rat in my life — as the vocalist said warming up: me, me, me.)

I claimed an empty coffee cup and filled it from the pot on the table.

Ivan asked, "How is your little girl doing?"

Him, I would have considered marrying . . . but so far, the widower had shown only middling interest in my potential, which I found strange (his lack of interest, not my potential).

Not wanting to spend too much time talk-

231

ing myself — otherwise I'd never hear what these old goats knew — I put on a truncated bus-and-truck performance of the show I had given Junior and Henry earlier, leaving out the improvisational improvements.

When I'd finished, Vern remarked, "Poor Joe . . . kid's never been right since coming home with battle fatigue."

Harold barked, " 'Poor,' my foot. Sees a little action overseas, then gets discharged on a Section 8. That softie doesn't know what *real* shell shock is."

And, neither did Harold. During the War to End All Wars, he'd never left an army base in Georgia. Of course, in his defense, the Nazis and Japanese never did make it past Atlanta.

Ivan, however, who had seen plenty of action at Guadalcanal, came to Joe's defense. "Let's not forget that that boy *voluntarily* enlisted — which is more than can be said about most young men these days — *and* he served honorably in the Gulf War." He paused, adding quietly, "No one knows a soldier's breaking point . . . not even the soldier himself."

That drew silence, and we all sipped our coffee. I admired Ivan's touching defense of Joe, but silently cursed him for throwing a wet blanket over the conversation. I had dirt

I needed to mine!

So, directing my question to the group, I asked, "Why wasn't Walter Yeager ever a member of the Romeos?"

The men exchanged uncomfortable glances.

I waited, excited, sensing I'd hit a nerve.

Ivan cleared his throat, then said simply, "Walt was all right. He just didn't really fit in."

His answer, however, didn't ring true to me. I knew that several of the Romeos had been in the same graduating class in high school, sharing many interests, such as sports, music, and photography. And Walter had been a pal of theirs. Nothing wrong with my memory.

"In what way didn't he fit in?" I asked casually. "Surely you hadn't grown *that* far apart in the intervening years. . . ."

Ivan shifted in his chair. "Viv, frankly? I'd just rather not say."

"Why not?" I pressed.

Ivan shrugged. "Don't want to libel the dead."

"You can't libel the dead," I pointed out. "They're *dead*."

"Well, then," Ivan remarked, "I don't care to speak *ill* of the dead."

We had arrived at an impasse. But there

was no impasse that yours truly couldn't squeeze through, jump over, or go around.

Leaning in conspiratorially, I said, "Henry just told me about the time he treated Walter in the ER, and Walter had something he wanted to get off his chest. It seemed *terribly* important — sort of a dying declaration. Any idea what that might have been?"

Ivan half-smiled. "Doesn't sound very likely. Consider the source. I mean, did Henry say what it was?"

"Walter never got around to spilling the beans." I paused, then pulled out my ace and played it. "If any of you know something, you'd better tell me, before Henry makes up something *preposterous* while in his cups."

Harold muttered, "She has a point."

Vern nodded, "I agree." He looked at Ivan. "It's your story, Ivan . . . so you should tell it."

Ivan sighed. "I guess it won't do any harm at this late stage. . . . Hell, pretty much everybody involved is dead by now."

I reached across and patted Ivan's hand where it rested on the table. "Another good reason to set the record straight. As we grow older, such things do matter."

"All right," Ivan said, and shrugged a little. "It happened during the summer of

'42. . . ."

"That was a *wonderful* movie!" I said. "*The Summer of '42*? Did any of you see that film? So romantic. . . ."

"Viv," Ivan said, frowning. "Are you interested or not?"

"Sorry. Yes. Vitally. Go on."

Ivan continued, "This all happened a month after graduation, and a few weeks before Walter and I enlisted in the army —"

"And me, too," inserted Harold. "I'll never forget the day when —"

I kicked the captain under the table for interrupting, and he growled, "Hey!" What was wrong with these old fools with their short attention spans?

For a moment, Ivan seemed to lose his train of thought, or else was fortifying himself to continue on with his tale. Then he picked up the thread. "One night before we were to ship out, Walter and I went on a double date with two girls who'd graduated with us from high school. Opal — she was my date — and Ella Jane. . . ."

Opal I'd barely known back then, but Ella Jane I did, of course. Her mother and I had just spoken at the nursing home.

"Walter drove," Ivan was saying, "and we went to a movie, I think . . . not sure because, well, it *was* a long time ago . . .

and I guess we'd all been drinking a little. Hitting the ol' hip flasks?" Ivan smiled briefly, then cast his eyes downward. "The next morning, Ella Jane came around to my parents' house looking for me. She was upset. She said that after Walter dropped Opal and me off, he . . . well, there's no nice way of saying this . . . *forced* himself on her."

Well, my dears, this news came as a shock to me, especially since I'd had my own intimate encounter with Walter, and only a few months before this alleged assault, and he had been so considerate and tender, his first time and all. But, then, alcohol hadn't been a factor.

Ivan was saying, "I . . . I didn't know what to do. . . . I guess I should have confronted Walter. . . ." He hung his head again. "And I was overseas by the time word got to me that Ella Jane had killed herself. So, you see, Vivian, why I — *we* — didn't care to have him in our group."

I said, "You *could* have done something when you got back, Ivan."

Ivan laughed dryly. "What? Accuse a returning war hero of an assault that may or may not have happened three years earlier, with a girl who was no longer living? Remember, I only got Ella Jane's side of the story. She killed herself, and that shows a certain instability. Who's to say her story was even true?" Ivan shook his head sadly. "But bottom line? I didn't really *want* to know."

Harold and Vern nodded, understanding. Once a boys' club, always a boys' club.

Suddenly, I wondered if Grace Crawford knew that her daughter might have been sexually assaulted — and by whom. Or had the girl kept her terrible secret to the very end?

What *was* it Grace had said? *Do unto others as they do unto you?* Had the elderly woman orchestrated Walter's death from her nursing home bed? If so, why had she waited so long?

And was she strictly confined to that bed, or was she mobile? Some old women, even lacking a driver's license, have been known to jump into a car and go off on one kooky quest or another.

Then something preposterous jumped into my mind: that the intended victim might have been *Chaz!* Thus doing to Walter what he had done to her: Take away what he had prized most, his newly found granddaughter.

I said out loud, "Then, Walter could have been murdered for a different reason."

Vern frowned. "Didn't he get killed for some valuable book? Anyway, that's what I heard."

"Me, too," Harold said. "That punk of a granddaughter of his did it, they say."

Defending the girl, Ivan said, "She *did* get released from custody. . . ."

"On a technicality!" Harold barked. "Ekhardt woke up long enough to get her off on a technicality, the old rascal."

Vern said, "Well, one thing's for sure . . . whoever has that book has to be the killer. It's worth thousands and thousands."

All of this was old news, and getting me nowhere, so I decided now was the time to reinforce my reputation as the all-knowing one around here.

I said quietly, "Joe had the book."

Which shook things up at the table.

When the Romeos' utterances had quieted, I told them about visiting Joe at the jail, and how the boy had denied poisoning Walter, but admitted to taking the book.

Ivan leaned forward thoughtfully. "If Joe *is* telling the truth, then there's only one logical conclusion."

"Which is?" I asked.

"Walter took his own life."

Harold scoffed, "What for?"

Ivan smiled sadly. "Guilt, maybe. Who

238

knows how Ella Jane may have haunted him over the years? But the likely thing is, Walter wanted to leave his money to his granddaughter before he ran through it himself. He was pretty sick, you know."

Harold said, "I can blow that theory out of the water — I heard cyanide was found in the girl's room. *That's* what the county attorney had on her."

Ivan shrugged. "I can't explain that, other than maybe Walter must have thought nobody would look there. He would've been certain his death'd be written off as a heart attack, given his long history of cardiac trouble. And the coroner, of course, having this information, perhaps seeing the pill case on the kitchen counter, would naturally jump to that conclusion."

"The coroner *has* seemed a bit befuddled since his divorce," I admitted. "Might be doing substandard work."

Ivan glanced at his watch, "Oh, hell — I've got to be at city hall in five minutes."

This announcement broke up our little group, and the men collected their checks. We walked out into the chilly late afternoon air together.

Ivan's blue Caddy, parked directly in front, was sporting a bright yellow ticket. He snatched it off the windshield, and said,

"That's what my meeting is about — getting rid of these damn things!"

"Ah!" I said. "Serenity without parking meters would truly be a paradise." Plus, I was running out of slugs.

Harold touched my arm. "I'd give you a ride home, Viv, but I drove the Jeep, and have Vern with me."

I assured the captain that I already had a lift home, and hurried off to catch the trolley.

Once aboard, I asked Shawntea if she would be so kind as to go off-route and take me to the convenience store by the trailer court in South End because they simply had the *best* day-old donuts, and she willingly complied.

While the trolley idled in the store's parking lot, I went in and strode up to the cashier, Claire, a young, weight-challenged girl with pimples, whom I'd talked to last night on the phone (Claire, not her pimples).

"Do you have my order ready, dear?" I asked.

She smiled, showing braces, "Yes. It's right here." The girl bent beneath the counter, and produced a white sack.

But as I reached for the package, she pulled it back, saying, "You're *sure* you

240

know Justin Timberlake?"

I gave her my most sincere smile. "Of course, dear . . . I told you that we're related. My mother was a Timberlake."

She beamed and the braces glinted in the overhead light. "I want the photo to say, 'Claire darling, I'll never forget our special night together' . . . and then he signs his name, okay?"

"Yes, dear. Justin will write exactly what I ask him to." I'd forged tougher signatures.

Then I bopped back out to the trolley with my sack.

I would like to leave you, dear reader, with one more funny trolley story, involving the town's little person, Billie Buckly, whose grandfather was a Munchkin in *The Wizard of Oz;* I'm sure I still have sufficient word count left, and Brandy certainly wouldn't be so mean as to cut me off in mid—

MOTHER'S TRASH 'N' TREASURES TIP

Possession is all ten points of the law. If someone is holding an item you want, it is theirs to purchase until they put it down. However, if I jostle them, and they drop it, and I get to it first, it's mine. If it should break, well, who *dropped* the thing, anyway?

CHAPTER NINE:
INSECURITY TAPE

Mid-morning, I was released from the hospital with orders from my doctor to take it easy for the next day or two, which suited me fine, because I'd gotten stalled halfway through a boxed set of the final season of *Veronica Mars,* so this gave me a chance to finish the series uninterrupted.

Even though Tina had sweetly offered to rearrange her work schedule at the Tourism Office so she could drive me home, I asked Peggy Sue, who had a bridge game at the country club that she would have to miss. Okay, maybe that was a little vindictive on my part, but I really did want to see if I rated higher with her than cards and social climbing.

Or maybe I didn't want to know. Fifteen minutes past the pickup time, Sis still wasn't there, leaving me cooling my wheelchair wheels curbside. I was getting unreasonably angry when she finally rolled up in her monstrous van.

"Terrible traffic" was her only excuse. Lots of traffic jams in Serenity, mid-morning. A real madhouse.

Still, with all due sisterly pleasantness, she put my meager belongings in the backseat while I climbed in front, as an attendant came out to retrieve the wheelchair.

Then we slipped away in silence.

After a block or two, however, the strain between us was too great for her (I wasn't about to speak first) and Peggy Sue began to jabber about family plans for Christmas. Then she was detailing the latest knick-knacks she'd bought for the ever-growing Department 56 Christmas Village that consumed one end of her living room.

"Tiny Tim and his whole family," she was saying with what struck me as faintly hysterical happiness. "The picture-perfect picture of a perfect Christmas!"

"Yeah, they had it great back then, in England. Hung holly all over the work-houses."

"Well, it's just a fantasy."

"Right. A happy family Christmas. That's a fantasy, all right."

"What is your problem, Brandy?"

"Were you *ever* going to tell me you're my mother?"

Sis slammed on the brakes, whose screech was like a scream, and the car following us did the same, brakes also squealing, and the car behind it, too. If you slammed on your brakes at the edge of a canyon, the echo effect would have been similar.

I guess being seated in a moving vehicle, with Peggy Sue behind the wheel, was not "the right kind of time" Dr. Hays had advised in broaching the subject of my true parentage.

Wearing the expression of a clubbed baby seal, Peggy Sue pulled the van over to the curb — the other startled drivers going by us — and she turned a distressed face toward me. "Who *said* I was your mother?"

"We'll get to that . . . *are* you?"

Peggy Sue's eyes returned to the windshield, her hands on the wheel, as if she were still driving, but she really wasn't going anyplace. Then her head slowly bent to the steering wheel, brown arcs of hair covering her face, and her shoulders begin to heave as she sobbed.

I guess I should have felt something. Compassion, sorrow, anger . . . *anything.* And you'd like me better if I had. But the truth is, I didn't. Maybe it was the antidepressant blocking my emotions, or the residue of the hospital painkiller . . . but I just let her sit there and sob.

When Sis finally raised her head, her eyes were smeared with makeup. Which is why, these days, I always use waterproof mascara.

I said, "Sorry," and shrugged. "Timing a serious discussion has never been my long suit."

Peggy Sue plucked a tissue from her expensive plaid Burberry bag and dabbed her eyes. Then she said, "No, it hasn't been. But you do have a real knack for picking the most inappropriate moment to go for the jugular."

I lifted my eyebrows; it was an effort. "We can do this later, if you like. After all, you've waited this long . . . what's another day or two?"

Peggy Sue winced at my remark, but then composed herself and took a deep breath. "No. We won't wait another moment. And I *do* understand why you're so bitter."

"Could you just say it? That you're my biological mother? You can fill in the blanks later, if you like."

"I am your . . . biological mother."

A little chill shook me. It was cold out, and the heater was off.

"As for filling in the blanks?" She shrugged. "I was supposed to go to France to study music after high school, but that summer I guess I was a little wild. Last summer at home, feeling like an adult now that I was out of high school." She laughed once, a harsh, icy, brittle laugh. "I was adult, all right. I got pregnant just like a grown-up."

I was frowning. "What do you mean, you *were* going to go to Paris? You *did* go! I saw the old snapshots of the Eiffel Tower and all that touristy stuff." I'd run across them in an box of family photographs.

"Yes," Peggy Sue said. "Most of my pregnancy was spent there. There was a family Mother knew, some theatrical connection, who put me up. Then, just before you were born, I flew back to the States and stayed with a relative in Maine."

I was smiling, but it wasn't a happy smile. "And I suppose, all the while, Mother was back here putting on a show, wearing a pregnancy pillow and flouncing around, letting Serenity know all about her 'late-in-life' baby."

Peggy Sue actually smiled a little. "At least neither one of us had to see it."

"What a performance *that* must have been."

Peggy Sue nodded. "Then, when the time came, Mother came to Maine —"

"Where she had 'her' baby." My fingers made air quotation marks. I hate it when people do that.

Sis nodded again.

"So. Who's my real dad?"

Peggy Sue stiffened.

"Oh, come on." I laughed dryly. "You had to know that'd be the next question out of me."

"He was just a boy."

"That much I'd worked out."

"A boy from my class. His name was Steve McRay."

"Was?

"He died in Vietnam while I was in Paris, where the peace talks were. He . . . he didn't know I was pregnant. Something very wrong about that, me in Paris, him in some awful jungle."

"You think? And you never told him?"

Sis shook her head.

"Why didn't you?"

She blinked at me a couple of times. Then she shrugged. "Because . . . well, I didn't *love* him."

"So I was the result of a lousy one-night stand back in hippie days? Make love not war? Or more like, make love, then war?"

"Please don't be this way. It's really tragic — the war was almost over, Steve was one of the last to die over there." She gave me a sharp look. "Anyway, it wasn't that way at *all. . . ."*

"How was it, then?"

She fell silent for a moment, then said, "I don't think I'm going to go there. You know why, Brandy? I don't think you're anybody to be judgmental about ill-advised one-night stands. At least *I* had the excuse of being young."

This was an overt dig at the way my marriage had broken up after I made a really dumb, drunken move at my ten-year high school class reunion. She was hitting below the belt, but I probably deserved it.

So I moved on. "How . . . how did this Steve McRay die?"

Peggy Sue swallowed thickly. "He was a gunner in the tail of a helicopter. They had the highest fatality rate in that awful war, tail-gunners. Mom wrote and gave me the news."

Peggy Sue's husband's face came unbidden to my mind's eye. I blurted, "Does Bob know?"

She shook her head again. "Only Mom . . . and now you."

"I beg to differ," I responded liltingly.

Peggy Sue raised one perfectly plucked eyebrow. "You mean, Mother didn't tell you? I know you two have gotten close since you came home. . . ."

"No — she's stayed mum, so to speak. But it is impressive — this has to be the longest she's ever kept a secret! No, Sis — you'd think I might have done the math, and thought about the unlikelihood of Mother having me just about when her menopause should have been kicking in. But I was a blissful idiot."

"So who told you?"

"Somebody sent me an anonymous letter."

Sis paled with alarm. "Oh, hell. Who . . . who do you think it was?"

"I have a pretty good idea," I said, smirking, "that it was your dear friend Connie Grimes. It arrived not long after she and I had that little dustup at Ingram's department store."

The front windows were fogging, so I cracked my side.

Peggy Sue frowned, saying more to herself than to me, "But what kind of proof could *she* have . . . ?"

I grunted a little laugh. "Gee, I wonder. How about your actions around her for the last thirty years?"

She frowned, truly confounded by my remark. "Whatever do you mean?"

I snorted once. "Are you kidding? You've been her faithful little lapdog for as long as

I can remember."

Her eyes and nose flared with indignation. "I have not!"

"Oh, *please!*"

Peggy Sue folded her arms, and her chin went up in its familiar defensive posture. "I don't treat Connie *any* differently than any of my other friends."

I let out another laugh. "Oh, really? What about the time you switched football tickets with her so *she* could sit on the fifty-yard line? Or when you took back that expensive dress because *she* wanted it? This was back before she gained a little weight, say, a cow's worth. And I seem to remember a canceled trip to Bermuda because *she* —"

Peggy Sue cut in. "I was just being a good friend!"

I gave her my best Clint Eastwood squint. "And what has that loathsome monster ever done for you, except make your life miserable?"

"That's simply not true!"

"It's simple *and* it's true . . . not to mention that that beast treats Mother and me like dirt —"

Sis huffed her own laugh. "Well, is it any wonder, the way you two act sometimes?"

"Thanks for making my point. Your 'friend' rags on your mother and your sister, or daughter depending on your point of view, and who do you side with? Elsie the Cow."

"That isn't fair."

"No. It isn't." Then I got back on point, pointing a finger at Sis. "Listen, I don't want Mother to know that *I* know. . . . I couldn't handle her theatrics. Could you?"

Peggy Sue shuddered and shook her head, once.

"Besides," I said, "*you* made the decision thirty years ago about how things were going to be, and I don't see any reason for them to change. You're to remain my sister, and Bob is my brother-in-law, and Ashley's my niece, and Mother is . . . well . . . Mother."

Peggy Sue searched my face for a long moment, then said, "All right. If that's the way you want it."

"It is." Then I narrowed my eyes and I held up a lecturing finger, as if she were the wayward child and I the stern mother. "Except for one thing — I expect you to start behaving like a supportive sister, and not a disappointed mother, which is how you've always treated me." I paused, adding, "You gave up the right to mother me a long, long time ago."

Her eyes tightened just a little. But if

Peggy Sue felt hurt, she otherwise buried it.

"All right, Brandy," she said. "But it's got to be a two-way street. You haven't exactly been supportive of me, either. You're condescending and cruel and far more judgmental than I've ever been."

I couldn't deny that.

"Deal," I said, and stuck out my hand.

"Deal," she said.

And my biological mother and I shook on it.

"Maybe it's about time we accept each other for who we are," I said. "Warts and all."

Peggy Sue smiled and nodded, and started the van.

"By the way . . . did *you* name me Brandy?"

Sis shot me a disparaging look. "Me? Name you after a kind of liquor? Hardly."

"What name did you want?"

"Chastity."

I gave her an appalled look, and then we both began laughing, laughing so hard she had to pull over again until we'd both wiped the tears from our eyes.

Mother, wrapped in her raccoon coat, was waiting for us on the porch as Sis pulled her van into the drive; Mother waved animatedly, and we waved back, smiling for her benefit.

I thanked Sis for the ride, then got out, and stood in the drive watching Peggy Sue back out in to the street. I felt pretty good, considering. A page had been turned.

"Hurry up, dear!" Mother called to me. "Everything's ready inside."

I could only guess what that meant, although I had a fair idea. Ever since I was little, whenever I'd been seriously sick or injured, Mother had put on a private little party for me. This consisted of the two of us watching a movie together (choose one or more: *Ferris Bueller's Day Off, Monty Python and the Holy Grail, Caddyshack, Meatballs,* and, newest on the list, *Waiting for Guffman,* although Mother doesn't find that movie quite as hilarious as I do). Mother would also make a delicious frosted cake, and popcorn balls, and, more than often, I'd eat too much and get sick all over again.

I was halfway up the porch steps when Sushi came flying out the front door, yapping in joy at my return. I picked Soosh up, snuggling my face in her soft fur, and she — in her excitement — peed on the front of my ski jacket.

Welcome home!

Inside, Mother held me out with both

hands, her eyes huge behind her lenses as she searched for any defects, the way she'd look for cracks in a piece of carnival glass.

"You seem fine, dear," Mother concluded, with no mention of the piddled-on coat.

"I am," I said, removing the thing. "A little sluggish, maybe."

"Peggy Sue didn't want to stay?" It was unclear whether Mother was disappointed or glad.

"She thought she could still make her bridge game."

"Well, then," Mother said, and clapped her hands. "It will be just us Three Musketeers. . . . Showtime in ten minutes!"

I had to admit I was looking forward to watching one of my favorite comedies with Mother, whose laughter was surprisingly genuine and as contagious as a cold, but I was pretty sure Musketeer Sushi would last only as long as the food held out.

I went upstairs, took a quick shower, then slipped on some comfy gray sweats. Below, I could hear Mother clomping around, punctuated by what sounded like furniture legs screeching, and I could only wonder what in the world she was up to.

When I came downstairs, Mother was standing in front of the French doors of the music room, beckoning me to hurry. Sushi was dancing at her feet, caught up in the excitement.

I couldn't imagine what Mother had planned for my homecoming — a gathering of my best gal pals, perhaps champagne and caviar, maybe a male stripper — but what I saw entering the music room wasn't even close.

I turned to Mother, aghast. "You made me a *clubhouse?* What am I, twelve?"

She had taken the Duncan Phyfe dining room chairs, formed a semicircle, and thrown a blanket over them.

"I would say eternally eleven," Mother said with a hurt, stricken look. "I just thought it would be fun for watching our movie — after all, the Queen Anne couch isn't terribly comfortable."

True. Victorian furniture was apparently originally designed to weed out the nonserious suitors. (Even as an adult, I always sat cross-legged on the floor for my at-home televison viewing.)

"Is there room in there for all three of us?" I asked.

"Of course!" Mother folded back a corner of the blanket for a door. "Come and see. . . ."

I bent and looked in. Mother had dragged in cushions and pillows along with a buffet of goodies stored in stacked Tupperware containers.

"Well . . . it *does* look cozy," I admitted.

Mother smiled. "Then why don't you and Sushi get settled while I start the movie?"

Sushi had already beaten me inside, settling on one of the pillows nearest the food, natch. I got comfortable on my side, and watched Mother through the opening while she inserted a tape in the player, then crawled into the playhouse to join us, her knees creaking as she came.

"Are you ready, dear?" she asked, the remote aimed at the TV like a cowboy with a Peacemaker.

"Yup."

The movie began, the opening shot being the outside of a convenience store gas station.

"What *is* this?" I asked. "*Clerks*?" I'd never seen the cult hit, but knew it took place at a 7/11-type shop.

Mother gave me a cat-that-ate-the-canary smile.

"Oh, I *know*," I said. "This is that indie movie shot here a few years ago — the one about a convenience store robbery."

Mother's smile turned even slier, which only made me irritated.

"Well, what *is* it?" I asked. There still had

been no credits, the opening shot of the gas pumps going on forever!

"Security cam footage," Mother said smugly. "From outside the South End convenience store."

"*What?* Why? How the heck did you get it?"

"Never you mind," she sniffed. "The point is, *this* tape will reveal who killed Walter Yeager, because we can see every car that goes in and out of the trailer park."

I sat up. "But, Mother . . . we already *know* it was Joe. I hate to admit it, but the evidence —"

"We're about to *look* at the best evidence in this case," Mother said, shaking her head vigorously. "I spoke with the boy yesterday at the jail. Walter was already *dead* when he got there! That means someone *else* paid Walter a visit, sometime earlier that morning. All Joe did was impulsively snatch up that rare book."

I considered that. Could Mother be right? Much as I hated to admit it (and didn't, not out loud), her gut feelings were often on target.

I asked, "How many hours are we looking at?"

"Oh, not many."

"Define 'not many.'"

"Only about four."

"Only about *four?*"

"Yes, dear — from when the store opened that morning at six until Joe arrived some-time after ten."

"Oh, brother . . . that's gonna *take* a while. . . ."

"Think of it as a double feature, dear," Mother said cheerfully, ever the pragmatic lunatic.

Mother produced a legal pad and pen from beneath one of the pillows, and handed them to me. "Here."

"What's this for?"

"So you can make notes."

"What kind of notes?"

She looked at me like I was daft. "Why, the cars that go in and out, of course. Now, this is serious detective work, so just relax and have fun."

"There could be hundreds of cars!" I gestured to the TV screen. "And I can't tell what color they are, from that black-and-white tape. Honestly, Mother, this is a waste of time."

Her nose twitched, like a rabbit detecting a skunk in the neighborhood. "So that's your attitude? Don't you want to prove that your friend Joe didn't do it? Do you have so many friends that you can afford to cast one to the fates?"

"Well, of course I'd like to help clear Joe," I said. I nodded toward the screen again. "But maybe all we can prove is that he *did* do it."

"If he did do it, dear, we have to tell the police. I hope you're not asking me to withhold evidence."

I sighed. What could I do with this woman?

"Start the show," I said.

We proceeded thusly: Mother watched the tape, calling out "Pontiac Grand AM — in," or "Ford truck — out," while I wrote it down. Sometimes, Mother wouldn't know the make of the car, and would stop and rewind the tape, and I would take a shot at identifying the vehicle. Then, after a half hour or so, we switched jobs — me watching, Mother writing. But fifteen minutes into my shift of watching, I heard a snore and looked over to see Mother asleep, her head resting on the thinnest possible pillow: her legal pad.

I paused the image, and was thinking about taking a snooze myself when the doorbell sounded.

Sushi, who had also been conked out, gave a yap, and Mother woke with a snort.

"Want me to get it?" I asked, stopping the tape.

"No, dear, it could be a package for you for Christmas that I don't want you to see. The mailman hasn't been here yet. He's way behind on his deliveries."

Now, I happened to know that I was getting a new pair of ice skates, because she'd told me not two minutes ago (Mother talked in her sleep). But I didn't burst her bubble.

"Fine," I said, "I'll take a food break."

Which caused a dilemma for Sushi.

Mother had mentioned "mailman," and he always gave Sushi a dog treat, but then again I had uttered that magicest of magic words: "food."

The doorbell ringing again, however, was too strong a conditioned reflex for the pooch, and she made a dash for the front door. Mother crawled out of the clubhouse, grunting and groaning like a felled elephant trying to get to its feet.

I reached for the container of yummy Danish cake. A minute or so later, I was nosily licking frosting off my digits when a pair of black shiny shoes beneath neatly creased gray trousers appeared at the blanket door of the clubhouse.

"Brandy . . . ?"

I froze, a sticky finger in my mouth.

The trousered legs knelt and revealed a starched white shirt, followed by the stupefied face of Chief Tony Cassato.

Mortified, embarrassed beyond belief, I could think of nothing to do except bring the chief down to my childish level.

I said, "You can't come in without the password."

"What's the password?"

"Pee-Wee's Playhouse."

"Okay. Pee-Wee's Playhouse . . . although I would have thought Mickey Mouse."

"Wrong generation. Too young for Annette, too old for Britney." I scooted over to make room for the chief, who — and I could hardly believe my eyes — had started to crawl in.

"Can't wear shoes, though," I stopped him. "Sorry, it's a rule."

Tony sat back on his haunches, began to undo the laces. "Any other rules I should know about?"

"Normally, it's no boys allowed. But there's an exception for chiefs, usually Indian, but you get in on a technicality."

"That all?"

"Well, there's absolutely no admonishing, criticizing, lecturing, or otherwise upsetting the clubhouse owner — namely me. I'll let you know if you break any other rules."

"Okay." Tony was inside now, and sat cross-legged, his head poking at the roof of the blanket.

I said, "You are by far the most prestigious guest we've ever had in the clubhouse. What brings you here?"

"I knew you were getting out of the hospital today. Just wanted to see how you're doing."

"How does it look like I'm doing?"

Tony glanced around. "Not sure that blow to your head didn't rattle a few marbles. I hope this was your mother's idea."

"Of course. She still treats me like a child."

"I wonder why."

I frowned. "*That* would be considered admonishing. Sarcasm is admonishing. I can get you the rule book, if you insist."

"Sorry." He reached out and touched my nose. "Sorry. Some stray frosting. . . ."

"Is it off?"

He nodded.

I gestured to the food — or what remained of it. "Would you like something to eat? You can have cake with my finger-marks on it, or popcorn balls that Sushi licked. The latter is probably a little more sanitary."

"Nothing, thanks."

Sushi trotted in at the mention of her

name (or cake or popcorn balls) and stood on Tony's thigh, tail wagging. Then she got up on her hind legs and gave his cheek a wet, pink-tongued kiss, before settling down in the space between his knees. She had a soft spot for the chief, associating him with Rudy, the K-9 drug-sniffing dog, the love of her life.

"How's Joe doing?" I asked.

"Out of lockup, but in the psychiatric pod."

Back when I was respectable and responsible, I had helped initiate the separation of the mentally ill from the general prison population at the new jail.

I said, "Joe's in a lot of trouble, isn't he?"

Tony responded, "If by that you mean weapons in a state park, resisting arrest, kidnapping and assault —"

"I *won't* press charges!"

"You have no choice," Tony said flatly. "He's transgressed against the city of Serenity and the state of Iowa."

"I didn't hear you list murder."

The chief shook his head. "No. That's not on the list . . . at the moment."

I asked uneasily, "You *did* find the cyanide pills?" I didn't want to add "attempted murder" to Joe's litany of troubles by telling the chief my friend had tried to force one on me.

Tony frowned. "If you mean the capsules in his duffel bag, they were analyzed as gelatin."

I gaped at him. "You mean the kind of stuff people take to grow their *nails* out?"

He nodded.

And I laughed. Then I laughed some more — so hard, in fact, tears of laughter ran down my face. Then the laughter tears turned to real tears and my body shook uncontrollably.

"Brandy, what is it?" Tony asked.

"Joe said it was —" I choked, and tried again. "He tried to make me —"

"Good God. . . ."

"He said we couldn't be taken *alive.*"

Alarmed, the chief slipped an arm around my shoulder, and I put my head on his chest and bawled.

After maybe a minute I calmed down, and pulled away, leaving his white shirt not so crisply pressed.

I sniffed, "I guess I hadn't dealt with that yet."

Tony dug into a pants pocket and gave me his handkerchief.

I sniffed again, "You know, I already have two of these you gave me. . . ."

Tony grunted a little, then said, "You'll be all right?"

"Yeah. Fine."

He checked his watch. "Look, I've got to go. . . ." He seemed to hesitate.

"I'm fine . . . *really.*"

He nodded.

Sushi, sensing Tony was leaving, got out of the chief's way so he could put on his shoes.

I crawled out of the clubhouse with him and we stood in front of the TV.

I said, "I'll see you out. . . ."

"No need." He was already on the move, but paused at the French doors to the music room and glanced back.

"By the way, that security tape? I want it this afternoon. I'd take it now, but we're short on manpower. Let me know if you find anything interesting."

My face turned beet-red.

Then, as he strode past Mother in the living room, I heard him ask her, "Justin Timberlake?"

What was *that* about?

After the chief had gone, Mother made a beeline to me.

"How did *he* know we had that tape?" Mother asked astonished, her eyes-behind-the-glasses big and unblinking.

I smirked humorlessly. "He *is* the top cop around here. And what's this about Justin Timberlake?"

Mother sidestepped my question with a grunt. "I categorically *detest* that man!"

"Justin Timberlake?"

"No! Anthony Cassato! He's hiding something!"

"Well, he seems to value our input on this case," I said. "Otherwise he would've immediately confiscated our tape."

Her frown disappeared. "On the other hand, I've always known he has some wonderful qualities."

Mother's opinion could turn on a dime, just like her thought processes.

"You two were in there a long time," she said slyly, with a nod toward the clubhouse. "Did he kiss you?"

"What? No! Why would you ask that?"

"No slap and tickle?"

"Mother!"

"Dear . . . please. Surely you know the man's in love with you."

"Now that's just ridiculous."

Mother shrugged. "Yes, but then there's no accounting for some men's taste."

"I meant ridiculous even for you!"

"I'm far too old for Chief Cassato, dear."

I took a deep breath. Let it out. "Can we

please get back to the tape?"

"If you wish . . . but let's use the chairs. If I bent back down and crawled in the clubhouse again, I fear I might never get back on my feet."

While I dismantled the clubhouse, Mother rewound the tape. Then we settled into chairs, me holding the pad, my pen poised for recording.

"Oh, damn!" Mother said.

"What?"

"I went back too far. . . ."

The outside lights of the convenience store were on, indicating it was dark.

"It's the night before," I said. "See the time code at the bottom of the screen?"

Suddenly Mother shut off the tape.

"What now?" I asked, irritated. "We're *never* going to get through it if you keep taking a bathroom breaks!"

"I'm too tired to finish."

Say again?

Mother was *never* too tired, and she never left *anything* unfinished.

She stood, then retrieved the tape from the machine, and handed it to me. "Go ahead and take this to Chief Cassato."

"Oh, all right," I grumbled. "What a waste of time!"

Mother turned on her heels, crossed the

living room, and trudged up the stairs. In another moment, I could hear the creak of her bed above me.

Well, she *was* getting older — and probably a good five years older than she claimed. And I wondered if this was a defining moment, perhaps the beginning of her decline, when she could no longer push herself as hard as she wanted.

My cell phone on the coffee table trilled.

"Hi," Tina said cheerfully. "Sorry for the short notice, but can Kevin and I take you out to dinner this evening?"

Had they come to a decision about the baby?

"Sure. What time?"

"Oh . . . about seven? We'll try that nice new Thai place, and then we can sit and, you know, talk this whole thing out."

"Cool."

Teen and I talked for a few minutes about what we were going to wear, but it was a pointless conversation because neither of us ever kept our word about such things.

I went upstairs to Mother's room to tell her of my evening plans, and found her seated on the edge of her bed, a book in her hands. I sat next to her.

"What's that?" I asked. "Your high school yearbook?"

She nodded. I looked at the page she had open.

"Is that you at the prom?" I pointed to the lovely statuesque blond girl in a strapless pink gown, dancing in the foreground of the crowd.

"Yes," Mother said.

What a dish she'd been!

"And that's Walter?" Her partner's back was to the camera.

"He was such a gentleman that night. . . ."

I stroked her arm. "Is there anything I can do for you?"

"No, dear. I heard you on your phone. I'm glad you're going out tonight."

"I can stay if you want me to . . . ?"

"No, I want you to go. I'll be fine."

I hesitated; Mother was unusually subdued and untheatrical for, well, for Mother. Perhaps it was best for her to spend some time alone with her memories.

"Won't be back until after midnight," I informed her. "Are you *sure* you won't need me?"

"Of course not! *I'm quite all right.* And should I want you, I'll call your cell."

"Promise?"

"Promise."

I was already out into the hallway when

Mother called, "Oh, dear? Will you be driving?"

"No!" I called back. "Tina and Kevin are picking me up."

Mother said something like, "That's nice, dear," and had my mind been on her response, instead of thinking about what I was going to wear, I would have realized that Mother was *not* all right.

Not by a long shot.

A TRASH 'N' TREASURES TIP

Most flea market dealers expect buyers to haggle a bit, and have built this age-old process into their prices. The polite way is to ask, "Is this your best price?" And the dealer will usually offer a ten-percent reduction. If you dicker any more, however, you've insulted said dealer, and he/she would rather throw the item into a vat of boiling lead than see you get it.

Chapter Ten: Fair Grounds for Murder

Mother has made an exceptionally good case that she should be allowed a second chapter, for the undeniably good reason that I wasn't around for much of it.

I go on record as stating that this does *not* establish a precedent.

I, Vivian Borne, took it upon myself to solve the murder of Walter Yeager for two reasons.

First, I could no longer count on Brandy to be my faithful little Watson; as you have seen, the child had become a basket case, and had I involved her in my attempt to apprehend said murderer, she might have gotten us both killed. And second, because the events that follow happened to me, and me alone, meaning that I not only have a right to write this chapter, but to do so *without* a word-count limitation to cut me off in midsentence!

As you may have surmised, I indeed saw

271

something damning in the convenience store's security tape that I did not share with my daughter; this happened only after I had accidently rewound it to the night *before* Walter was killed. So it was pure luck (or perhaps God Himself) that took Brandy out of the house, enabling me to act upon my suspicions without endangering the dear girl.

As soon as she left — looking quite lovely, I must admit (if only Tony Casatto could have seen her like *that* that afternoon, he might have proposed on the spot!), I marched over to the downstairs phone.

When the individual I suspected of murder answered my call, I said, "I have proof that you poisoned Walter Yeager, but I'm prepared not to go to the police, as that would serve no worthwhile purpose, now that that innocent girl Chaz has been freed. Instead, I suggest we discuss a possible future, and very profitable, business venture."

I suggested further that we meet somewhere private at, say, nine o'clock tonight, inside the building used for the flea market at the fairgrounds where this all began. Then I warned the individual, quite cleverly I thought, not to try any tricks.

"I'm leaving behind a letter for Brandy," I said, with the confidence of a veteran performer, "stating where I am going and with whom I'm meeting."

And I hung up.

After dressing warmly in my emerald velour pantsuit, I took from my bedstand drawer the small tape recorder I sometimes used for running my play lines, and tucked it in a pocket of my raccoon coat. Then I sat at the kitchen table to write out my figurative insurance policy, i.e., the brief letter to Brandy telling her what I was up to, with whom, and where.

Then it took only a few more minutes to find Brandy's spare car keys (which she'd hidden in a collectible — and therefore never used — cookie jar high in a cupboard, once again underestimating me), after which I strode fearlessly out into the bitterly cold night. (My Audi was as dead as Jacob Marley, since our last cold snap.)

The wind was whistling through tree branches and rustling snow and rattling icicles as I approached the garage. At first, the Buick did not want to start. But I coaxed it to life, and soon I was cruising down Elm Street with all the aplomb of a legally licensed driver.

You see, I hadn't driven for quite a while, due to a series of silly misunderstandings between me and the traffic department;

consequently, at the intersection of Elm and Mulberry, I slid on some ice and coasted through a stop sign, narrowly missing a red Mustang. The driver rolled down his window and yelled at me — a most un-merry, un-Christmaslike greeting for this holy time of year. After that, I was more careful, even crossing the dangerous bypass with nary a mishap, and the rest of the drive was uneventful.

As I approached the darkened fairgrounds — not even an outdoor security light was shining — the sprawling, one-story main building, where I'd won many a blue ribbon, seemed dwarfed next to the venerable wooden grandstand, silhouetted against the night sky like a massive beast waiting to pounce.

I parked in front of the main building, shut off the engine, and stepped out.

Franklin Peabody was a part-time maintenance man at the fairgrounds; he owned a farm nearby, and it was easy for him to keep an eye on things out here during the slow winter months. Now, I happened to know that Frankie hid a spare key to the building on the ledge above the front entry, because he had to get it once after accidentally locking some of us Red Hat girls outside during the pie-baking contest. (Which I won with my own mother's strawberry and rhubarb recipe.)

So, before you could say Bob's your uncle (strange expression, considering Bob really was Brandy's uncle), I was inside the building, the vast room still, long rows of flea market tables bare, a far cry from a few weeks ago, when a boisterous crowd threaded through aisles as vendors hawked colorful wares . . . and where Walter had so proudly introduced me to his granddaughter Chaz, happily outlining their new life together.

I shivered, partially from the memory but mostly because the heat wasn't on, and I could see my breath making little ghosts that evaporated so that another could materialize. At a wall panel of switches, I turned on just the front few ceiling lights, then walked back into the semidarkness, creeping along the rows of tables, the folding chairs tucked squarely beneath them (Frankie Peabody was a neatness-freak).

When I arrived at the table that had been used by Walter, as best I could estimate anyway (the chamber seemed so different when empty), I pulled out a chair, sat behind it, to wait just beyond the more fully illuminated front area of the hall.

After half an hour, just as my toes were

going numb, the door swung open, then banged shut, and the murderer strode forward, stopping under the glare of those front overhead lights, eyes searching beyond into the ever-darkening interior. The eerie overhead lighting made shadows and dappled the planes of the familiar face darkly, making something always friendly before seem sinister now.

"Yoo-hoo, Ivan!" I called. "Over here!"

The ex-mayor's head swiveled in my direction, and he cupped one hand over his eyes, the better to see me. He was wearing a cap that matched his plaid hunting jacket (the implications of which did not escape me), and I watched him closely as he approached, finding the right aisle and coming down.

I had placed a single folding chair in the aisle, on the other side of my table, as if we were about to do business in the flea market. And, as far as he was concerned, we were, weren't we?

"Sit," I said, gesturing with one hand, while with the other, in my coat pocket, I turned on the tape recorder, its tiny click muffled by the raccoon fur.

Ivan plopped down with a little laugh and tossed his cap on the table and folded his arms. His tone was genial. "Honestly, Vivian, I've had some kooky calls from you in my time, but this one takes the cake! If you had something on your mind, couldn't you've picked a place that served hot coffee?"

I didn't smile, but said, "You know my flair for melodrama, Ivan. How could I resist returning to the scene of the crime for the denouement? Or should I say, return to the *seed* of the crime? Isn't this where your thoughts of murder first sprouted?"

Ivan sat back, meeting my eyes. He had a smile that wasn't much more than a line with gently upturned ends; his eyes had a coldness worse than anything the outdoors could serve up.

He said, "I have no idea what you're talking about, Vivian, except that you seem to have the ridiculous notion that *I* had something to do with Walter's death. I know all about your pretensions of being an amateur sleuth. I only accepted your invitation because it's better if we have this out privately, and don't embarrass *you,* and put *me* in a position of having to take legal action against an old friend. So go ahead — how did you get this crazy idea in your head?"

I smiled. "You have every right to know how I arrived at my conclusions. I don't have any desire to embarrass you, either. We're at an age where, in all honesty, we only have a few years left, and not even good ones. I have no desire to make your final years unpleasant, though I would like to make my own last act a really rewarding one. That's why I think we can do some business."

Ivan spread his hands and said impatiently, "Well, then?"

I leaned on the table, tenting my fingers. "Let us first go back to the night of the flea market preshow. Walter was here, center stage. *You* were downstage center. *I* was stage left —"

Ivan interrupted. "Jeez Louise, Vivian — could you skip the theatrical lingo just for once?"

"I'm merely setting the stage. . . ."

The thin smile evolved into something sarcastic. "Okay, I get it. I was there, he was there, you were there. . . . *So what?*"

"You don't have to be *rude,* Ivan."

"Oh! Sorry! By all means take your time. I had nothing better to do tonight than drive out here to the middle of nowhere and sit in a freezing cold room and hear you babble a bunch of nonsense about me murdering somebody I barely *knew.*"

I pursed my lips. "You knew Walter once,

though, didn't you? Very well indeed."

He said nothing.

"You were near the table when Walter made a remark about being relieved his secret was out — referring, of course, to his illegitimate granddaughter, Chaz. *You* replied that some secrets were best kept secret because of unhappy consequences . . . which, at the time, I thought to be merely an idle comment."

Ivan shrugged. "I don't remember saying any such thing. But even if I did, it was just so much conversation. I didn't mean anything by it."

"Oh, but you did! It was a very pointed remark, certainly a threat to Walter to keep his own counsel about some *other* secret. In fact, you may have felt Walter had *meant* his remark to be overheard by you — giving it a double meaning only you would discern."

Ivan studied me, then sat forward and said, "You know all about why I dropped that louse as a friend, Vivian, way back in the war years. I told you in detail about that double date we had all those years ago. . . ."

I nodded. "I heard a version carefully crafted by you. Revisionist history, isn't that what it's called?"

Ivan's eyes narrowed. "What the hell do you mean by that, Vivian? I gave you the straight scoop."

"Aw, but what were you scooping? Ella Jane was your date . . . *not* Opal. She was with Walter. And *you* drove that night."

"Hogwash!"

"No. Not hogwash, nor poppycock. A photo in our high school yearbook confirms it. Granted, I had to use a magnifying glass to be sure . . . but that *is* you, in the background, with an arm around Ella Jane. And as I thought back about it, really thought back, it finally returned to me: You continued to date her throughout the summer, didn't you?"

"We . . . we may have dated. But we broke up and she started going with Walter and —"

"No. You don't go double-dating with somebody who's taking out the girl you just broke up with, not back then you didn't, anyway. It was *you,* Ivan, who took advantage of that poor girl that night . . . and that's the secret Walter Yaeger had on you."

"You're guessing. And you *are* going to get yourself sued, you silly pretentious witch."

"I may be all those things. But you're a rapist, Ivan. It's not something you can stop being, either — it's like being a murderer. You murder in your youth and you never do a single bad thing after that, but on the day you die, maybe on your ninety-fifth birthday, you die a murderer. And you, Ivan, will die a rapist."

His face had turned white.

"Ella Jane was too ashamed — or perhaps afraid — to tell anyone what you'd done to her, and then she went off to college as planned, only to discover that she was pregnant. And with you off at war, and with nowhere to turn, she hanged herself. That's right, isn't it? It's hanged, not hung?"

Ivan stood and thrust a trembling finger at me. "Vivian, you meddling old gossip, if you go around spouting that nonsense, I *will* sue you for slander! I *swear* I will!"

I smiled up at him patronizingly. "Please sit down, Ivan . . . I told you on the phone I had proof. So suing me is out of the question, since the truth is the best defense. But you needn't be upset. We'll work something out."

His face went slack. He shook the finger at me, but then dropped into the chair, slumping there, glowering at me.

"Let's not get ahead of ourselves," I said. "After Walter implied he would need paying off, which is of course blackmail — what was it that he said? He wanted to give Chaz things, 'and that takes money'? That was when you decided he had to die. After all, you had to protect your good name and social standing. So you left the flea market and drove to his mobile home, where you —"

"Hold it," Ivan said. "Just how did I get in? If you're going to spin stories, Vivian, you have to make them believable. The newspaper said the police said there were no signs of a break-in."

"Everybody has a spare key hidden around. How do you think I got in *here*? May I go on?"

"By all means," Ivan said archly.

"Where was I? Oh, yes, once inside the trailer, you found Walter's weekly pill box — that was another clue, by the way, you mentioning that the other day, with the Romeos — and you replaced the contents of the capsule Walter would take the next morning with cyanide." I raised a finger. "Then — just in case his death might appear suspicious to the police or coroner — you hedged your bets by planting some of that poison in Chaz's bedroom, to implicate her."

"Wouldn't that just have confused the issue?"

"No. If they accepted the death as accidental, there would be no search. If they were suspicious, there would be a search, and you'd tie any suspicion to a granddaughter who was both a stranger in town and, shall we say, a trifle rough around the edges."

Ivan clapped his hands. "Bravo, Vivian, that's quite a story, even for you. You should really consider producing it at the Playhouse. Only, one small item — *where* in the hell would *I* get a hold of cyanide?"

"I must admit that stumped me at first, because it *is* rather difficult to obtain, these days." I shrugged. "But not so difficult, years ago, when it was used in photoprocessing — when you and Walter and some of the other fellas had a photography club. And you still have your old developing room in your basement, don't you, Ivan?"

The ex-mayor tilted his head, and his smile dripped condescension. "So far, Vivian, all I've heard is wild speculation — nothing that even vaguely resembles 'proof.'"

The time was right to play my high card. "I have a security tape that shows you driving into Walter's trailer court *after* you left the flea market."

Ivan's smile froze.

I went on, "And while that might not be enough to bring an indictment against you for murder, it certainly will be of interest of the police, not to mention the attention of the public. And the kind of investigation the professionals will mount will make that of an amateur sleuth like myself seem . . . amateurish?"

Ivan stared at me with hard, barely blinking eyes. Then he said flatly, "Let's hear it, then, Vivian. What's your proposition?"

I adjusted myself in my chair. "First, let me say I'm not greedy. I know you have no love for a blackmailer, as what happened to Walter Yaeger attests. What I propose is a partnership between two adults, who understand that neither of them is, well, perfect. You've heard that the Playhouse is up for sale? Well, I'd like to buy it, only. . . ."

His eyes had a disturbing deadness now. "Only you're short on capital."

"I do have *some* funds . . . but not enough to swing the down payment. So my proposition is this: You go into business with me, and I'll give you that tape."

(But not the one running in my coat pocket.)

Ivan seemed to be considering my offer, so I added, "If you prefer, you could be a *silent* partner. . . ."

He stood, this time slowly. "No, Vivian, *you're* going to be the silent partner . . . utterly silent, which is the dream of everyone who has ever known you."

And from his jacket pocket he withdrew a revolver, a small thing with a short snout that shouldn't have looked at all formidable but was perhaps the most frightening thing I ever saw.

Nonetheless, gentle reader, I was pleased and proud of this development — Ivan threatening to kill me with that gun, why, it was as good as a confession! The only problem being that the gun couldn't be "seen" on the tape recorder, so I had to perform something of a radio play, saying, "Ivan, put down that gun!"

Pointing the weapon at me, he sneered and said, "I always knew your snooping would get you into serious trouble someday. And quite frankly, Vivian, I must say I'd rather go into business with Medusa herself than the likes of you. At least Walter Yaeger wasn't a mental case."

Now that did hurt a bit, and I responded, "Why, Ivan, I always thought you were rather fond of me."

His laugh was also a sort of snort. "Would you like to know what I *really* think? You're a conceited, crazy old busybody."

I arched my eyebrows. "I take exception to that. I am not *old*." You're only as old as you feel, anyway.

"Well, let's just say," he said, "that today is as old as you're ever going to be."

I stood and said indignantly, "Might I remind you of the letter I left behind in case something untoward should happen to me?"

Ivan reached inside his coat. "You mean *this?*" He tossed my letter to Brandy on the table. "Thoughtful of you to mention it on the phone. And thoughtful of you, also, to leave a key under the mat. You're so right — everyone *does* leave a spare key hidden around."

I admit that my confidence was shaken; I may have been an amateur sleuth, but I was a professional actress, and this was not going according to the script.

And suddenly I was sorry that I hadn't involved Brandy. I could have used that spunky little lady about now!

Spreading my hands, I tried reasoning with him. "Killing me will only compound your problems, Ivan. I have reason to believe that the security tape will find its way to the police, with or without me. And my suspicious death will be linked to Walter's, and a *real* investigation will turn you up just like I did."

He shook his head. "I don't think so — not if your death looks like an accident.

Hand over your car keys, please."

"What are you planning?" I stalled.

"The keys, Vivian."

I got them out of my pocket and put them on the table.

He reached for them. "What else have you got? Cell phone?"

I put it on the counter and he took it, dropped it in a pocket of the hunting jacket.

He nodded, then gestured forcefully with the little barrel of the small, nasty gun. "Let's go. We're going to check out the Christmas lights — out in the country."

I wasn't exactly sure what Ivan had in mind for my "accident," but I was willing to bet it began with the butt of his gun making potentially fatal contact with my skull.

And Vivian Borne was not about to let that happen — if she had to die, she would die trying . . . trying to escape, that is.

I said, "I'm sorry, Ivan. I'm not going anywhere. You're going to have to shoot me, and deal with a very uncooperative corpse."

He shrugged. "Your cooperation really isn't needed, dead or alive, you harridan."

And he came around the table.

As quickly as I could burn the sugar cookies on Christmas Eve, I grabbed my folding chair and hurtled it at Ivan, buying me precious seconds to scurry deeper into the otherwise darkened hall.

But Ivan, instead of chasing after me in the dark, ran over to the wall panel and began turning on more ceiling lights, trying to flush me out, one bank of spotlights at a time.

As the lights flickered on — threatening to reveal my hiding place in the far corner near the red glow of an exit sign — I weighed my options, which were few. I could either stay here and be chased around the vast hall, or take my chances outside in the cold.

I bolted out the exit door.

Almost immediately I regretted my decision.

The already bitter wind had increased, making the dangerous wind chill even more deadly. Unwittingly, I had created the perfect "accident" for Ivan: Unless I found shelter immediately, I would most certainly freeze to death.

With difficulty, I ran in the snow toward the grandstand, the nearest structure where I might find cover from the freezing wind. I stumbled under the wooden bleachers, crouching as I moved in, advancing as far as I could beneath the steps. There I huddled on the ground, which, thankfully, only bore a dusting of snow, yet the bitter wind still reached me with its icy fingers, tweaking my ears and nose.

My situation was looking bleak indeed, when my half-frozen fingers found a Bic cigarette lighter among the debris that had fallen through slats in the bleachers. Saying a little prayer, I flicked the Bic, and it worked! Gathering all of the paper trash around me, I stuck the pile under the bottom step, and lit it. The result was rather amazing, even for me. . . .

There was a crackle, and a pop, then a big *WHOOSH!* as the ancient wood quickly caught fire. The flames, fanned by the wind, spread quickly upward and outward, and I had to fall back fast to keep from getting burned. Within minutes the grandstand, a structure apparently consisting of unwitting kindling, was a fiery inferno, painting the night orange, cutting through the darkness with claws of flame.

If *that* didn't catch somebody's attention, I didn't know what would!

I stood a safe distance from the blaze, wondering where Ivan had got to . . . what was he doing? What was he thinking? Was I still in danger, or had he run off?

I was contemplating my next move when the help I had hoped to attract arrived sooner than I had expected: A police car, lights flashing, siren blaring, barreled down the main drive of the fairgrounds. I waited until the car came to a slippery stop between the main building and the roaring, dying grandstand, then hurried toward it.

And I nearly dropped my upper plate when the passenger door flew open and Brandy jumped out. She ran toward me, with Officer Lawson on her heels.

Brandy's face was red with anger (or maybe from the glow of the fire).

"Mother!" she shouted. "You *know* you're not supposed to drive!"

"I don't need a hearing aid, dear," I said. "We'll discuss my confiscating your vehicle later. Officer Lawson, there's a murderer with a gun on the loose!"

He frowned at me. "What is it *this* time, Mrs. Borne?"

"I am sane and this is real! Ivan Wright just confessed to me that he killed Walter."

The sirens and clanging of fire trucks became apparent in the background and grew and grew.

"What kind of nonsense is this?" the snippy officer asked. "Did you start this fire, Vivian? What's going on?"

"I told you, you obstinate whippersnapper — Ivan, our esteemed ex-mayor, is a murderer!"

That was when Ivan came running from the direction of the main building.

"Vivian," he said, out-of-breath when he reached us. "Thank God you're alive! I was afraid you were caught in that fire. . . ."

"How touching," I said dryly.

Ivan looked from Officer Lawson to Brandy. "I'm afraid Mrs. Borne has really gone off the deep end this time," he said, his voice laced with seeming concern. "She asked me to come out here, and then tried to extort money from me to invest in that silly Playhouse. . . ."

I clapped my hands. "Excellent performance, Ivan! I had no idea you could act — I really should have used you in some of my plays. But, unfortunately for you, this little improvisational monologue will not hold up . . ." I withdrew the recorder from my coat pocket. ". . . because I have everything that you said on this tape."

Ivan looked at the officer. "She's out of her mind, I swear this is all delusional nonsense. . . ."

"And this," I said, waving the recorder, "along with the security footage from the convenience store, will be enough to implicate you in the murder of Walter Yeager."

Ivan looked at Brian, expecting his support, but instead the officer said, "As a matter of fact, sir — we do have some questions we'd like to ask you at headquarters, and perhaps now would be the best time to —"

Ivan's face went slack.

I said, "Careful — I told you, he has a gun! It's small, it could be in his pocket!"

But then it wasn't in his pocket; it was in his hand, small and black and frightening-looking, ready to spit more fire into a night already yellow, orange, and red.

We froze.

Then Brian slowly put one hand up, palm out, like a traffic cop, while his other hand hovered over his own holstered weapon.

"You need to put that gun down, Ivan," Brian said.

The barrel of Ivan's revolver moved from Brian, to Brandy, to me.

"Vivian Borne," the ex-mayor said, silhouetted against the glowing sky, "I hate you. . . ."

Ivan's hand came up and there was a quick, sharp crack as he fired a bullet into his temple.

Then he dropped to the ground like a child making a snow angel.

Brandy here.

Mother and I sat in the back of Brian's

squad car as if we were the prisoners, and maybe we were. He was out there helping keep bystanders away as the old grandstand turned into cinders. Three fire trucks were expending lots of energy and plenty of water, but the only thing that could be accomplished was putting out the blaze — the damage had been done.

Mother said to me, "How ever did you find me, child?"

"I tried calling you from the restaurant," I said, "and when you didn't answer our phone or your cell, either, I went home and found my car gone!"

I was furious with Mother. I knew she'd been through a traumatic episode — of her own making! — but, really, I could have put her across my knee and spanked her.

But instead I kept filling her in: "Then I got a hold of Brian, and all he had to do to find you was follow the traffic accident reports."

Mother frowned as if she had no idea what I might be referring to, the eyes big and innocent behind the oversize lenses. "What on earth do you mean, dear?"

"You didn't notice you'd caused a seven car pileup on the bypass?"

"I did no such thing," she huffed.

"Then you knocked over a mailbox just

down the road, so we knew you were coming here. Couldn't you have just dropped bread crumbs?"

She raised a finger. "The mailbox I *do* remember. What was it doing, positioned so close to the street like that?"

"Mother, how did this fire start? I hate to ask, but . . . did *you* do that?"

She shrugged grandly. "What else could I do? Ivan had my cell phone, and I didn't have a flare."

Oh, she had a flare, all right. Mother definitely had a flare.

MOTHER'S TRASH 'N' TREASURES TIP

The earlier you arrive at a flea market, the greater the selection, but the later you come, the better the bargain. If you're specifically looking for good furniture, get there before the rooster crows — like the bladder, it's the first thing to go.

CHAPTER ELEVEN: NEW YEAR'S REVOLUTION

Since the late Ivan Wright was the major suspect in the murder of Walter Yeager, the county attorney shut down the investigation. And, although rumors swirled around Serenity like a shook-up snow globe, no official statements regarding the former mayor's involvement in the homicide were issued. Mother said Ivan still had enough local political ties to cause embarrassment, should his misdeeds come to light. But I think a general sadness had settled in among Ivan's friends and acquaintances, who could see no reason to unearth long-buried secrets dating back as far as the 1940s.

On the other hand, Chaz and her attorney, Mr. Ekhardt, might well think it was time to get out the shovels. A strong possibility remained that Chaz could file a civil suit against Ivan's estate for the wrongful death of her grandfather. Mother, on the hand

(and she does have her sources), doesn't think that will go anywhere — she insists that eventually it will come to light that the state of Ivan's financial affairs, at the time of his suicide, was dire — that he was deep in debt.

"Wait and see," Mother said. "You'll find that certain of our esteemed local financiers have, over the years, made substantial loans to our respected former mayor, enabling him to maintain a lavish lifestyle beyond his actual means."

Speaking of Mother, she was (you may or may not be relieved to hear) not charged with arson for burning down the grandstand at the fairgrounds. She gave a statement that, after being chased at gunpoint out into the night by a murderer, she had fled into hiding beneath the bleachers, where she soon became convinced she would freeze to death if she didn't start a small fire to "warm my poor hands by."

So the fire was ruled accidental by the authorities (if not by me).

She met my skepticism with a typically theatrical dismissal: "Considering how quickly that ramshackle old structure went up in flames, why, that fire was a blessing in disguise! The best Christmas gift I could ever have given the city of Serenity."

"Really."

"Indeed! Imagine if a spark had turned those dry old boards into a conflagration while the seats were filled with the behinds of Serenity citizens taking in a home game! Why, the loss of lives could have been catastrophic, not to mention the number of lawsuits the county would face. Now the fairgrounds will have a safe, state-of-the-art grandstand, attracting more events and crowds, which should easily offset the cost of the new construction."

This seemed ridiculous to me. But around town, Mother was (no kidding) a heroine in the eyes of many.

But not Tony Casatto.

The chief, furious that Mother had once again taken the law into her own hands, refused to speak to her, spurning her phone calls and impromptu visits at the station. This frustrated Mother to no end, as she hated being out of the loop — any loop.

Christmas came and went, just Mother and me and Sushi and a handful of gifts and nonstop Christmas movies on both the 24th and 25th — the original *Miracle on 34th Street* (accept no substitutes), the Alastair Sim *Christmas Carol* (ditto), *Christmas Story*, *Christmas Vacation*, and *It's a Wonderful Life*. We dispensed with the clubhouse, however, and Mother sat on the couch while I lounged on throw pillows.

Jake, now eleven, arrived for a few days before the new year, looking a little taller, his round face having lost some of its baby fat (sorry, son). I had always thought he looked more like me than Roger, but now I could see that Jake's features were beginning to morph into those of his dad. (And Roger even sent me a generous gift certificate for Ingram's.) We had a second Christmas — I got Jake some Japanese video games, and he gave me the new L.A.M.B. perfume by Gwen Stefani — and I gained five pounds eating all those goodies, again. Had to make sure they were all out of the house by January first, didn't I?

One overcast, cold morning right before December gave way to January, I drove Mother out to the Sunny Side Up Nursing Home to see Grace Crawford. I remained respectfully out in the hallway (but within hearing distance) while Mother quietly — and with surprising dignity and compassion — informed the bedridden woman of who had been responsible for her daughter's death so many years ago.

"Thank you, Vivian," Grace said with very little emotion in her voice. "But I'm afraid I've known about that for a long, long time."

Mother was stunned momentarily into silence, then managed, "You *knew* Ivan had gotten your daughter pregnant?"

"Oh, my, yes."

"Did . . . did Ella Jane tell you?"

"Yes, but not face-to-face. I received a letter from Ella Jane the day after she died. Some might call it a suicide note, but to me it was a loving farewell to her mother."

"But you . . . then you *didn't.* . . . ?"

"Bring the matter to the attention of the authorities? Would that have brought my daughter back? Would Ivan have even been charged with anything? The word of a returning hero against that of a dead girl, who was so mentally unbalanced as to take her own life?"

"I see." Mother, being an Old Testament eye-for-an-eye kind of gal at heart, seemed disappointed in Grace's turn-the-other-cheek New Testament attitude.

Then Grace Crawford chuckled. "Not that I didn't *eventually* do something with the letter."

"What?" Mother could barely contain her excitement.

"I used it to feather my own nest . . . for many years." Grace gestured with a bony hand around the nicely decorated private room. "Who do you think has been paying for me to stay here? I certainly didn't have the money. But Ivan did." She cackled again. "Having that vile man squirming on the end of a hook like the worm he was — year upon year — was much more satisfying than having him serve the kind of short prison stay he would have gotten . . . *if* he would have received one at all, back then. But prison wasn't the point — *reputation* was. Respectable citizens, mayors of cities like Serenity, don't take advantage of young girls."

Mother drifted out of the room, looking a little shell-shocked. I was a trifle surprised myself — Grace had turned out to be an Old Testament gal, too, hadn't she?

But in the car, Mother lowered her head and began to cry. I got a handkerchief out of her handbag and gave it to her. It was quite touching right up to where she blew her nose with a definite *honk.*

"I thought you were all for getting even," I said.

"What that woman did wasn't getting even, it was taking advantage. She 'feathered her nest' on the bones of her baby. How horrible. How terrible. And Ivan — no wonder the years twisted him, facing one blackmailer after another . . . and I was the last, wasn't I? The one who sent him over the edge."

"He was an awful man."

"He was flawed. I can't justify what he did to Ella Jane — who would, who could? But we weren't there to see it. We weren't young boys facing war, either, like he and all the others were. Perhaps Ivan might have come back and made amends through public service — I believe he tried to — but the past wouldn't let him."

"Keeping secrets buried," I said, "can be costly, Mother."

"What . . . what do you mean, dear?"

"Nothing. Just what I said."

On New Year's Eve, Brian and I went out to dinner at a new French restaurant on the bluff overlooking the frosty Mississippi. Brian, looking handsome in the brown cashmere Armani sweater I had given him for Christmas, seemed cheerful, although a little distracted, which I assumed was due to a heavier-than-normal work schedule at the police department over the holidays.

I wore a black satin Donna Karan dress that I'd been saving for just such an occasion, and I tried to act happy even though I was miserable, because I hadn't told him yet about my offer to carry Tina and Kevin's baby, which my friends had gratefully and joyously accepted three weeks ago.

After dinner, we went back to Brian's small apartment, which he had cleaned for the occasion, and he popped open a chilled bottle of champagne — which almost always cheers me up, but this was one of the "almosts" — and then, because the room didn't have a romantic fireplace, he put a DVD of one on his big-screen TV. (Who couldn't love this guy?)

As we sat together on his couch, sipping bubbly, basking in the DVD/TV crackling fire, Brian, his arm around me, finally said, "Brandy . . . we need to talk."

Had he noticed that our seemingly perfect evening was off kilter?

I said slowly, "Yes . . . I have something to tell you."

"And I, you." He removed his arm from around me.

This sounded serious, and I twisted my torso to gaze at him. "You go first. . . ."

"Ladies first."

"No. . . . You started this."

Brian sighed, gazing at the TV fireplace. "We're going to have to stop seeing each other for a while."

Whatever I might have guessed he'd hit me with, this was not it!

I reared back. "You're breaking up with me?" Nobody has *ever* broken up with *me!*

Not counting my divorce, anyway. I couldn't help feeling crushed.

I sputtered, "It's Mother, isn't it? She drives you crazy, right?"

"No. I mean, yes, she drives me crazy . . . but then she drives everybody crazy, and . . . that's not the reason."

I waited.

Brian swiveled on the couch to face me. "It's . . . it's Bonnie, my ex-wife. . . ."

Oh, no! The dreaded ex-wife! He was still in love with her.

But Brian was saying, "It's our older girl. She's really having some problems."

"I'm sorry. . . ."

"It's an eating disorder. Pretty serious. Very serious, actually . . . and Bonnie is freaking out, and my younger girl is a mess, too. I have a responsibility, Brandy. My girls are going to need me."

I blinked a couple times, processing that. By "girls" did he mean his daughters, or his wife and daughters? But I couldn't bring myself to ask. What I did ask was: "But . . . I thought they lived in Wisconsin . . . ?"

Brian nodded. "And I'll be making regular weekend trips there to see them. For counseling sessions, and just . . . being there."

"Oh."

"It's a Dad thing." He touched my face.

"Let's think of it as a hiatus, okay? Still, I can't expect you to wait for me . . . and I'd understand if you, well, decided to move on."

Date others. But where would *I* find someone as sweet as Brian? And how could I compete with a family that needed him, a family he'd made before he ever even met me? And how could I be mad at him for wanting to help someone he loved? Wasn't that what I was doing for Tina?

All I could do was nod numbly.

Brian cocked his head. "You said you had something to tell me, too. What was it?"

I waved a dismissive hand. "It was nothing. Really."

Why go into my surrogacy offer? Now that Brian was out of the picture. Maybe I'd write him a letter about it. I could always send it to Wisconsin. . . .

Brian got to his feet. He looked pale, even stricken. "I . . . I suppose you'll want me to drive you home now."

I looked up at him. "Not really. I hate to waste a roaring fireplace DVD and a perfectly good bottle of champagne."

And I pulled him down to me.

The following afternoon, to commemorate the beginning of a new year, Mother and I made a pact. We trooped outside to the backyard, dug a small campfire in the snow, and burned our raccoon coats. (The stench was terrible, and a few of the neighbors called to complain. But I had no regrets.)

Which brings me around to the "cast, crew, and others" party at our house after the first night of Mother's new Agatha Christie production, which opened to a packed audience.

Mother had been right about Chaz's acting chops: The funky little Brit was terrific in her role of the amateur sleuth, providing much-needed comic relief, most of it intentional. Mother, wearing dual hats of both director and actor, was similarly strong. Her part as the murder victim, although small, garnered gasps from the audience at the staging of a real car seemingly running her down on stage. (Chief Cassato, in the front row with other local dignitaries, appeared to enjoy the stunt maybe a little too much, but that could just have been my imagination.)

After the performance, our house was crawling with people (in a good way): cast and stagehands, friends and neighbors, and a few folks I'd never seen before, who probably spotted the party from the street and decided to cash in on the food and drink. (I would.)

Mother, tiring of answering the door, hung (or is it hanged?) a sign outside, borrowing words from that hippie song: WALK RIGHT IN, SIT RIGHT DOWN.

Among those dropping by to offer their congratulations on the Playhouse's latest hit were Tina and Kevin, though they didn't stay long, Teen feeling pretty tired after her first chemo treatment, though she'd made it through the play.

Right before she left, Tina asked, "Where's Brian?"

I hadn't told her yet; I hadn't figured out how. "He had something else tonight."

"Oh. Too bad."

Even Joe Lange stopped by. He seemed a little ill at ease, so I assured my old friend that all had been forgiven and forgotten, even though the lump on the back of my head hadn't quite receded.

"I'm going to stay on my meds, from now on," he said. "I promise."

"Same back at ya."

"You're not mad? You're really not mad?"

I gave him a hug.

"Roger that," he said with a goofy grin.

Just as the party was really kicking in around eleven, Chaz made a grand entrance on the arm of boyfriend Ben. She looked chic and sexy in a short red sweater dress, a departure from her usual all-back leather, her black hair changed to a softer shade of amber; Ben also had had a makeover, traveling from grungy to preppy, although truth be told, he seemed a tad uncomfortable in the very new clothes.

Knowing I should be in the kitchen dealing with dirty dishes, I buttonholed the pair.

I smiled at Chaz. "You look great. Radiant."

"Thanks, Bran," she said, smiling back.

I turned to Ben. "And that's a new look for you, too, isn't it?"

He blushed. I swear he did. "Chaz picked 'em out . . . and, well, I do what she wants." He looked adoringly at her, the poor whipped puppy.

"Yeah, well, 'e's goin' to college now, innit? An' I want 'im to look the part. First rule of actin', your ol' lady says."

That explained the Tommy Hilfiger clothes. "That's great!" I said, pleasantly surprised. "Where? Studying what?"

Ben grinned. "Community college . . . night classes mostly. I want to run my own auto-parts business."

"That's really swell." I looked at Chaz. "And what are your plans? After the play, I mean. . . ."

The girl screwed up her face in that ador-

307

able way. "Well, I can't say jus' yet . . . be busy with the new 'ouse, for starts, innit?"

My eyebrows went up. "You've bought a home?"

Ben said excitedly, "Chaz sold her trailer, and I sold mine, and we're gettin' a new double-wide."

I looked at the beaming pair and wondered if I'd ever been that happy.

"An'," Chaz interjected, "with the money we got from peddlin' the Ape Man book, we can fix up the caravan super nice!"

Mother had sneaked up beside us. "How *much* did you get?" she demanded, then, "I *wish* you'd consulted me, my dear!"

Mother often felt strongly proprietorial about things that were in no way hers.

Chaz tossed her head back. "Naw, Miz Borne, we got it sorted proper — forty thousand dollars! An' you know 'oo bought it?"

Mother and I shook our heads.

"That nasty bloke from the flea market!"

Mother gasped, "Not Harry Potthoff?"

Chaz nodded. "The very one. 'E's got a posh wife, now, yeah? Filthy rich, she is, and a right collector of books and that. And he ponied up the cash right and proper, or anyway *she* did."

Apparently, Pudgy had also been scouting

308

for a well-heeled wife.

Mother said grudgingly, "Well, you seem to have done adequately, my dear . . . but I'm sure a better price may have been possible if —"

I interrupted, "Why don't we let Chaz and Ben mingle, Mother. I'm sure there are other guests who'd like to offer their congratulations on Chaz's star turn."

And I took Mother by the arm and led her a few steps away.

"Let it go, Mother," I whispered. "What's done is done."

She went tsk-tsk. "Yes, I suppose — money under the bridge. But I *could* have gotten them *much* more, I'm sure of it! Why don't people ever learn to listen to me?"

"I'll get back to you on that. Just don't make trouble for those two. They're happy as clams."

She sighed deeply. "All right, dear. I'll let *this* one go. But remember — the clams in *Alice in Wonderland* were happy, too, and look what happened to them!"

Then Mother shifted into her hostess-with-the-mostest persona, flitting over to a group of new arrivals, and I disappeared into the kitchen to do a little scullery maid duty.

Noticing that we were out of clean glasses,

I was standing on tippy-toes to reach some on the top shelf of a cupboard when an extra pair of hands appeared to help me out, and a male voice said, "Let me get those."

I turned to see Tony Cassato, his black trench coat unbuttoned, revealing a crisply pressed blue shirt and gold tie.

Surprised by his presence, I could only manage, "Thanks."

"Where do you want these?" he asked.

"On the counter's fine."

The chief set the glasses down.

I said, "Nice of you to come to the play."

"It was fun."

"Right — particularly when Mother got run over."

He gave up a smile.

"Does your stopping by mean you're speaking to her again?" I asked.

He twitched a tiny smirk. "Yeah. I find it's better to keep the lines of communication open, where Vivian Borne is concerned."

"Ah — you're learning."

An awkward silence followed; then Tony cleared his throat. "I just dropped by to say . . ." He paused, looking uncomfortable, and I felt a quick chill, wondering if new charges were going to be filed against Mother.

". . . I'm sorry about you and Brian."

This was an incredibly un-chieflike thing for the chief to say; he had never even acknowledged that Brian and I were seeing each other.

I said, "You heard we broke up?"

"It's a small station. Word travels fast."

"Well, in Brian's defense —"

But Tony cut me off. "You don't have to tell me the details. Frankly, I prefer you wouldn't."

"Hey, he didn't just drop me, no matter what the department rumor mill says. He had a perfectly good reason."

"Hard to think what that could be."

That was a compliment of sorts, but I was on the spot. It was perfectly possible Brian hadn't told the chief about his personal situation, and that he'd be running in and out of state on his days off for a while. And it wasn't my place to tell him.

I plastered on a smile and tried to sidestep. "I wouldn't think who one of your officers was going out with, or not, would even get on your radar."

"Yes. Yes, it did. It's just that. . . ." Taciturn Tony was having trouble finding the right words. How the hell did he pull off interrogations, anyway?

He tried again. "I always like to know about anything that might affect the work of my men, who're out on the line every day."

Suddenly, I was pretty sure it wasn't Brian's welfare he was really interested in. . . .

Okay, I thought. Let's see how supportive the chief really is.

I said, "You may as well know something else — it'll be all over town soon — but my best friend's fighting cancer and she and her husband can't have kids. So I'm going to be a surrogate mother for them."

Funny. I could never have told Brian that in such a straightforward way.

Tony was nodding, saying, "Well, great. Well, that's great."

I smiled. "Yes, it is, isn't it?"

Mother flounced into the kitchen. Her face went from startled, to pleased, to smug in five seconds. "Oh, dear me . . . I didn't mean to intrude!"

And she traipsed out again.

Tony asked, "What was *that* about?"

I laughed a little. "Don't pay any attention to Mother. She has this wild idea that you and I might get together someday, and then she'd have access to all *kinds* of confidential information."

"Is that right?" he said with a one-sided smirk.

"I'm mentioning this so you won't get caught up in her matchmaking web."

Tony didn't say anything for a moment, then, "What if I don't mind?"

I stared.

"What I mean to say is," the chief said quickly, just a shade of embarrassment in his tone, "I really wouldn't mind, Brandy, if you and I were friends and not just acquaintances."

"Uhhh, I thought we *were* friends."

He nodded. "Good."

I nodded. "Fine."

What was *that* all about?

Tony shifted awkwardly, "Well. I guess I should be going."

I thanked him for coming to the cast party, and he nodded again, then left.

My mind whirling, I watched Tony weave his way through the crowd to the front door.

Was Mother right? *Was* Tony Cassato "sweet" on me?

Impossible.

And even if he were, a romantic relationship with the chief of police was one place I could not go. Mother would be absolutely intolerable! We'd be looking into every Serenity crime from shoplifting on up.

Peggy Sue entered the kitchen. She was wearing beige woolen slacks with a matching sweater set that I recognized from the winter Ralph Lauren collection.

Sis said, "You look beat, Brandy. Why don't you let me take over in here?"

Another shock. Peggy Sue, rolling up her cashmere sleeves to do dishes? When exactly had I gone through the City on the Edge of Forever portal into the alternate Brandy universe?

I asked, "What's Mother doing?"

"Enthralling her friends from the Red-Hatted League in the music room with the gruesome details of your latest case."

I grunted. "The party could go on all night. . . ."

As Peggy Sue replaced me at the sink, I ventured, "Peg. . . ."

Since I rarely called her that, she turned to look at me with interest. "What is it, Brandy?"

And I told her the whole spiel about the baby thing.

At the end, Sis raised her perfectly plucked eyebrows and said, "I would never under any circumstances do that to *my* body . . . but then, we're different, aren't we? So you have my blessing."

Not that I needed it; still, it did make things easier between us.

I said, "I have the first in-vitro procedure

next month." Then I warned her, "So you know there's bound to be talk."

Peggy Sue knew I was referring to her prized and protected social standing taking a hit because of her wayward sister, but again she surprised me.

"If my friends don't like it," she stated flatly, "then they're not really my friends, are they?"

"Could you go down to the basement with me?"

"Why?"

"I want to check and see if your pod is down there."

She laughed and so did I.

It looked like Peggy Sue and I really *were* going to have a different relationship now. Free of hostility and secrets.

"Thanks, Sis," I said, patting her arm.

Then she did something truly astounding: She kissed my cheek.

Upstairs, I found Sushi asleep on top of my bedcovers; the commotion of the party had been too much for her. She'd started out the evening yapping and dancing and yapping and dancing, but now she was spent. I kissed her furry little face, and she rolled over for me to scratch her soft tummy.

Also on the bed was my mail from the past few days, which a whimsical Mother had placed on a silver platter, because they were mostly bills. One letter, however, wasn't an IOU. It came in a plain white envelope with no return address and my name and address computer-printed.

I smirked. So, evil Connie Grimes was sending me a *second* poison-pen letter about Peggy Sue being my real mother, because the first one hadn't created the expected fireworks.

I tossed it in the corner wastebasket.

Then I had a second thought: I'd mail the damned thing back to her. I'd love to see her face, then!

I sat on the edge of the bed and opened the envelope, and the familiar typed words sprang forward: *WOULDN'T YOU LIKE TO KNOW . . .*

Only the last part of the sentence was completely different.

. . . THAT YOUR REAL FATHER IS A SENATOR?

I sprang from the bed, ran out into the hallway, and screamed, *"Peggy Sue!"*

Stay tuned.

A TRASH 'N' TREASURES TIP

When acquiring antiques as an investment, remember that the most valuable collections are the ones gathered through love and commitment. If you try to anticipate what will be collectible tomorrow, today you will fail. (Anybody want to buy a box of pet rocks?)

ABOUT THE AUTHOR

Barbara Allan is the joint pseudonym for husband-and-wife mystery writers Barbara and Max Allan Collins.

Barbara Collins is one of the most respected short story writers in the mystery field, with appearances in over a dozen top anthologies, including *Murder Most Delicious, Women on the Edge, Deadly Housewives,* and the best-selling *Cat Crimes* series. She was the coeditor of (and a contributor to) the best-selling anthology *Lethal Ladies,* and her stories were selected for inclusion in the first three volumes of *The Year's 25 Finest Crime and Mystery Stories.*

Two acclaimed hardcover collections of her work have been published — *Too Many Tomcats* and (with her husband) *Murder — His and Hers.* The Collins's first novel together, the Baby Boomer thriller *Regeneration,* was a paperback bestseller; their second collaborative novel, *Bombshell* — in which Marilyn Monroe saves the world from World War III — was published in hardcover to excellent reviews.

Barbara has been the production manager and/or line producer on *Mommy, Mommy's Day, Real Time: Siege at Lucas Street Market, Eliot Ness: An Untouchable Life,* and other independent film projects emanating from the production company she and her husband jointly run.

Max Allan Collins, a five-time Mystery Writers of America "Edgar" nominee in both fiction and nonfiction categories, has been hailed as "the Renaissance man of mystery fiction." He has earned an unprecedented fourteen Private Eye Writers of America "Shamus" nominations for his historical thrillers, winning twice for his Nathan Heller novels, *True Detective* (1983) and *Stolen Away* (1991), and was recently presented with the Eye, the Private Eye Writers of America's Lifetime Achievement Award.

His other credits include film criticism, short fiction, songwriting, trading-card sets, and movie/TV tie-in novels, including *Air Force One, In the Line of Fire,* and the *New York Times* best sellers *Saving Private Ryan* and *American Gangster.* Currently he is writing a series of novels for the top-ten hit TV series *Criminal Minds.*

His graphic novel *Road to Perdition* is the basis of the Academy Award–winning DreamWorks feature film starring Tom Hanks, Paul Newman, and Jude Law, directed by Sam Mendes. Max's many comics credits include the "Dick Tracy" syndicated strip (1977–1993); his own "Ms. Tree"; "Batman"; and "CSI: Crime Scene Investigation," based on the hit TV series, for which he has also written six video games and an internationally best-selling series of novels.

One of the most acclaimed and award-winning independent filmmakers in the Midwest, he wrote and directed *Mommy,* premiering on Lifetime in 1996, as well as a 1997 sequel, *Mommy's Day.* The screenwriter of *The Expert,* a 1995 HBO World Premiere, he wrote and directed the innovative made-for-DVD feature *Real Time: Siege at Lucas Street Market* (2000). A recent DVD boxed set of his films includes his award-winning documentary *Mike Hammer's Mickey Spillane. Eliot Ness: An Untouchable Life,* the film version of his Edgar-nominated play, has earned rave reviews and is available on DVD from VCI.

"Barbara Allan" live(s) in Muscatine,

Iowa, their Serenity-esque hometown; son Nathan graduated with honors in Japanese and computer science at the University of Iowa in nearby Iowa City, did post-graduate study in Japan, and now works in the video game industry, translating Japanese into English.

We hope you have enjoyed this Large Print book. Other Thorndike, Wheeler, and Chivers Press Large Print books are available at your library or directly from the publishers.

For information about current and upcoming titles, please call or write, without obligation, to:

Publisher
Thorndike Press
295 Kennedy Memorial Drive
Waterville, ME 04901
Tel. (800) 223-1244

or visit our Web site at:

http://gale.cengage.com/thorndike

OR

Chivers Large Print
published by BBC Audiobooks Ltd
St James House, The Square
Lower Bristol Road
Bath BA2 3SB
England
Tel. +44(0) 800 136919
email: bbcaudiobooks@bbc.co.uk
www.bbcaudiobooks.co.uk

All our Large Print titles are designed for easy reading, and all our books are made to last.